What others are saying about DEATH IN THE TRIANGLE:

"Wow... what an awesome read! Once I started reading, I was a captive and couldn't put it down as I was so anxious to see what happened next. It is a professionally written story that brought back tons of memories of my time in Vietnam. John nailed it!"

- Joe Fair, author of "Call Sign Dracula: My Tour with the Black Scarves."

"When reading *Death in the Triangle*, I could see all the faces, the sweaty jungle, hear all the mind-numbing yet terrifying sounds, smell all the wretched odors, and feel the deepest fears. You said it was fiction. It's too real to be that. Too honest to be that. A great sequel to When Can I Stop Running?"

- R Scott Ormond, author of "Shadow Soldier: Kilo Eleven."

"Once the soldiers set out on their patrol, the action is nonstop. Podlaski puts the reader right in the thick of the danger and action in this short story! It truly gives an outsider a better understanding of what the Vietnam War was like."

- Yvette M Calleiro, author of "The Chronicles of the Diasodz."

"In "*Death in the Triangle*" John Podlaski weaves another excellent tale of a small infantry unit, fighting in the lethal caldron of Vietnam's Iron Triangle. Follow Polack, Sixpack, Doc and other members of the 1st Platoon as they execute their difficult missions. Highly recommended!"

i

- Joe Campolo Jr, author of "The Kansas NCO trilogy" and "On War, Fishing & Philosophy."

"Death in the Triangle reveals a richly detailed universe in exquisite detail, just as I remember it, with its sights, sounds, and smells. This story begins right where *"When Can I Stop Running"* left off. The author is a great story teller and readers will bear witness to the physical and mental hardships these young men overcame to complete the mission. Highly recommended.

- Christopher Gaynor, author of **"A Soldier Boy Hears the Distant Guns**". His work also includes a feature story and photos in "Time Magazine."

"In *Death In The Triangle*, John Podlaski's third intriguing tome about the Vietnam War, John pulls you into the real experience of combat soldiers with his seat of the pants, painstakingly frank, truthful account of what real combat was like for our warriors. John, a decorated veteran of that war, tells the story of the daily trials and tribulations of a group of veterans, as only a person who has 'done that/been there' could.

John's down to earth, regular guy portrayal of those experiences, reflected and influenced in his writing by his personal memories, takes us to Vietnam and the Triangle. You'll cringe, weep, laugh, shudder, and feel this whole story like you were there; not wanting to set it down."

- Jerry Kunnath, outdoor writer Member of the Michigan Outdoor Writers association

DEATH

IN THE

TRIANGLE

A Vietnam War Story

DEATH

IN THE

TRIANGLE

A Vietnam War Story

By

John Podlaski

Janice J. Podlaski – Contributer
Nicole A. Patrick – Copy/line Editor
Nicole A. Patrick – Book Cover Designer
Printed in the United States of America

For Jan, Nicole, and Scarlett

God Bless America's soldiers – Past, Present,
and Future

Author's note: There were many military acronyms and slang terms used by soldiers during the Vietnam War which are included in this story. In case you are non-military or have forgotten over time, I've added a glossary of terms at the end of this book for your reference.

TABLE OF CONTENTS

Maps showing the location of this story…

The Iron Triangle is within the circled area

Note the triangle in the upper right

Chapter One

Sixpack (Sgt. Holmes) brushed the flap aside and entered the large green canvas tent that the First Platoon Wolfhounds called "Home" as the First Battalion built its new firebase dubbed Lynch. Inside, a heavy, musty odor permeated the air, most likely caused by the tent sitting in storage since the Korean War. To a newcomer, there was a rancid/cheese-like smell, almost overpowering to the senses; body odor from 30 unbathed soldiers. The men worked hard and sweated profusely since their arrival last week – digging holes, filling sandbags, laying concertina wire, building bunkers, patrolling, and going out on ambushes. Many looked forward to the portable showers scheduled to be erected later this week. In the meantime, everyone smelled the same and therefore nobody noticed the pungent odor.

The six-foot-four, muscular, broad-shouldered staff-sergeant was outfitted in his patrol gear. Battle suspenders draped his shoulders and held two smoke grenades, four concussion grenades, and two first-aid bandage packs hanging from embedded metal clips sewn into the material. The suspenders held up a weighted web belt encircling his waist. Attached were two ammo pouches with four 18-

round magazines in each and two canteens of water - one over each hip. An ammo bandolier draped across his chest – ala Pancho Villa, with seven 20-round clips in individual pouches. Sixpack's pockets on both his blouse and pants bulged outward, stuffed with C-Ration tins, a map, bug spray, a couple of flares, and other necessities he needed for the patrol. Completing the ensemble, a green boony hat covering his sandy colored hair, small tufts of curly yellow hair poking out from the sides; a green cloth towel straddling his shoulders; and an M-16 rifle gripped tightly in his right hand.

As the platoon sergeant moved along the center aisle, his tattered and bleached combat boots plodded through a trough of ankle-deep mud in the center aisle – thanks, in part, to the heavy overnight rain. The suction made it difficult to pull his foot free after each step, sounding like a plunger in a waste-filled toilet, while small whirlpools in the water above the muck marked his path. Sleeping soldiers lay in various poses on wood-framed green canvas cots along both sides of the swamplike aisle, making the noise unavoidable. These cots were quite uncomfortable for most over five-feet tall; the wood poles at both ends cut off circulation and numbed legs during most sleepless nights. Every fully clothed soldier still wore muddy boots with red caked mud resembling pie crust splattered across their trouser legs, almost reaching the knees. Some soldiers were covered with poncho liners against the chill of night. Others, who had been on duty all night, had simply laid on their stomachs on the taut canvas, using either poncho liners or arms as pillows. Light snoring complimented the outdoor sound of a waking firebase.

The greenish brown canvas side walls of the tent would soon be rolled up in preparation for the upcoming heat of the day. The tied rolls of tarp-like material usually hung suspended just above the top layer of a four-foot high wall of sandbags surrounding each of the five identical tents of the company. A gentle breeze flowed through the length of the bay from one end to the other. Rucksacks, helmets, weapons, extra ammo, boxes of C-Rations, and other personal items were stored against the sandbagged wall next to each cot, designating the personal space of each soldier. First Platoon's tent was the closest to the artillery batteries but farthest from the battalion Tactical Bunker and mess tent which stood near the center of the compound.

Last night, First Platoon's responsibility was to provide security for the firebase. Thirty-two members split duties: a single squad conducting an overnight ambush, two soldiers in a listening post, and the rest manning perimeter bunkers. Uninterrupted sleep was usually rare in the bush or in a firebase since watches took place in shifts. First or last watch provided the best chance of a decent night's sleep, but still not guaranteed when a 50% or 100% alert was required all night long. At daybreak, the war continued with new assignments. Sleeping in was a memory from home. Soldiers learned quickly to catch some z's whenever the opportunity arose, and many learned to fall asleep standing up.

Their LP reported many enemy soldiers stopping and moving past their location last night. Shortly after, several mortar rounds landed inside the firebase, putting everyone on high alert while the mortar and artillery batteries sought out the enemy mortar crew.

Less than an hour later, Rock's Third Squad blew its ambush and killed nine enemy soldiers, recovering a mortar base plate, 10 mortar rounds, 200 rounds of 7.62mm ammo for AK-47's, bags of rice, tins of fish and chicken, personal effects, cigarettes, official documents, letters and a map. The ecstatic intelligence group couldn't wait to scrutinize the bounty turned in at the TOC earlier that morning.

The final incident occurred a couple hours before sunrise. The LP reported movement to their front, reacting with grenades at the perceived threat of attack. The enemy soldiers turned out to be a family of rock apes, tossing large stones at them in retaliation for trespassing into the animals' domain. Updates of incidents occurring outside of the firebase usually circulated slowly, however, Polack (John Kowalski) and LG's (Louis Gladwell) experience on LP with the rock apes had spread like wildfire. Rock's ambush squad and the LP returned this morning to a barrage of jokes and teasing, making for a humble day.

Sixpack kicked the boots hanging over the end of the cot; clumps of dried mud dropped off and fell into the swamp causing splashes and rippling in the still water.

"Let's go, everybody up!" He kicked the next pair of boots and watched pieces of the red pie crust drop and splash. "It's 0830 hours. If you haven't eaten, get some chow, grab your shit and meet by the gate in 30 minutes."

Soldiers stirred and struggled to sit up, their movements slow and zombie-like. Complaints echoed throughout the tent.

"Bullshit, Sixpack. I just laid down."

"Yeah, none of us got any sleep last night."

"Quit your bitchin', man. We took fire during our ambush, lost a couple guys, and then had to pack up and move in pitch black darkness. And on top of that, we had to haul all the gook shit back with us."

"I heard that!"

"Can it!" Sixpack spat, causing everyone to suddenly stop. "We all suffered last night," he emphasized, "be at the gate in 30 minutes and don't be late!" Sixpack moved through the shallow portion of the channeled water brushing through the entranceway and leaving the tent.

The complaining resumed as soldiers gathered equipment and left the tent in small groups.

Polack and LG walked out together and headed to the mess tent for some breakfast. "I hope we don't hear any more shit about the monkeys last night," LG offered.

"Me neither, bro. I about shit my pants when that happened though."

"You and me, both, brother. That was my scariest night since being here."

LG walked with his head hung low, his boony hat still jammed down on his head with the brim resting on his ears: a gift from Sgt. Rock before going out to the LP yesterday. Prior to leaving the firebase last night, LG spent time working his 'do' which in his opinion was perfect, in the shape of a shiny bowling ball. His boony hat sat on top like a clown hat, swaying side-to-side with every step. When Rock reached him in line during the ambush squad's final equipment check, he pulled down on the brim of his hat so forcefully it captured all his hair and bottomed out on the top of his ears.

Polack glanced at LG's soggy hat, still on since last night. "Head hurt?"

"No, why?"

"I thought with your boony hat jammed down tight like that it might cause a lot of pressure around your head."

"Naw, I'm good. In fact, saved me some time this morning and I didn't have to rake it and get it in shape before leaving."

"It's bitchin'!" Polack stated sarcastically. "You should wear it like that all the time, G."

"You know Polack, you might be onto something there. If I buy a bigger hat, the man will never know how long my hair is. I'd keep growing it and then really fit in with the brothers when I get back to the world."

Both smiled and hammered their fists together in a mini dap.

LG and Polack hailed from Detroit and lived within four miles of one another. They played basketball at their respective high schools but never played against one another; Polack attended a Catholic school and LG played in the public school league. Named "All State" during his final two years, LG secured a college scholarship, but flunked two of his classes, revoking his free ride. Uncle Sam found him soon afterward.

At six feet tall, 170 pounds, Polack's normally fair-complected skin was baked to a dark bronze from the hot tropical sun. He sported medium-brown hair, somewhat bleached out now, and a light mustache, the hair slightly longer than regulation. This being his sixth month in-country, he was away from the main base camp and forward fire support bases for almost two months. Out in the jungles, personal grooming is low on the list of daily priorities. With no one to impress, nobody cares how they look. His shaggy hair was not an issue, at least not here at Firebase Lynch.

Louis stood a couple inches taller than Polack with a slightly lankier build. An African American, with light caramel-colored skin, a long and narrow face with a forehead lightly pitted with old acne scars. LG tried to grow a goatee since arriving in-country but only acquired a dozen or so half-inch long hairs spread across his chin. He checked his hand mirror daily, anxious for any signs of goatee progress, unwilling to give up on the plan. LG just began his fourth month in Vietnam and had been carrying the platoon radio since his arrival.

Both are generally involved whenever a pick-up game of basketball happens in the firebases or rear area during a three-day break from the bush. However, they always seem to be on opposing teams and have never played together.

The two men joined the line at the mess tent and loaded up on weak orange juice, runny scrambled eggs, leathery strips of bacon, and toast burnt on one side. They ate mostly in silence because of the limited time and left five minutes before they were to meet at the main gate.

On their way, LG broke away and headed to the Battalion CP where he joined four other soldiers to sign out PRC-25 radios and extra batteries for the patrol.

Polack carried his M-60 machine gun on the right shoulder, and with his right hand, held on to one of the extended front legs to keep it balanced. A feedbox with 100 rounds was attached to the side of the pig (slang for the machine gun), and Polack had 300 more wrapped around his waist.

The members of the First Platoon were gathered in a haphazard formation and loitered near the gate; 28 soldiers clumped together with weapons in hand, some wearing fatigue jackets, others, only sleeveless green t-shirts for the patrol. All four squads kept mostly to themselves, each clique engaging in separate group conversations.

Polack was a member of the First Squad. His mates, Frenchie, Wild Bill, Scout, Doc, and BJ were animated in their discussion about the upcoming patrol. All had worked hard during the week at filling sandbags and building fortifications within the new firebase. This was a welcomed change of pace.

When nearing the gate, Billie Joe (BJ), Polack's assistant gunner, left the group of waiting soldiers and hurried out to meet him. Outfitted like the others, he wore suspenders, an ammo belt, grenades, and an M-16 rifle, and humped another 300 machine gun rounds encircling his waist like Polack.

BJ from Alabama tried to be a 'good ol boy'. The newest member of the squad, he had only been in country six weeks. The men quickly nicknamed him 'BJ' and assigned him to Polack as an ammo bearer for the machine gun.

On his first mission, he fell asleep during the last watch out in the bush. The platoon was operating in the Michelin Rubber Plantation where a curfew existed between 1800 hours and 0600 hours. The last man was supposed to wake everyone at 0530 so they could disassemble their mechanical ambushes before the end of the curfew. An explosion woke them all at 0630 and they all worried that innocent civilians walked into the booby trap. When stepping out onto the trail, they found four dead VC soldiers, and others nearby fired at them while running away. The dead gooks saved both BJ and the platoon from dire consequences. Billie Joe was scared straight from that point on and had not fallen asleep on watch ever since.

"Is it true what they're saying that y'all threw grenades at a bunch of monkeys last night?" he asked sincerely when reaching Polack.

"Really?" Polack looked around and noticed smirks on many of the faces of those soldiers standing about. "We thought they were gooks!" he responded, loud enough for those nearby to hear.

"Hiding up in the trees?" somebody from the Fourth Squad asked.

"We didn't know they were in the trees."

About that time, LG joined them and did a shortened version of the 'dap' with BJ. As the greeting took place, small pebbles and stones landed at their feet.

"What the fuck?" LG said when a small rock hit his boot. He scanned the faces of his fellow soldiers from the platoon, but nobody smirked or looked guilty of anything, and none dared to meet his gaze in fear of laughing out loud.

Those in the First Squad watched intently as their 'Brothers' got a good-natured ribbing from the rest of the platoon.

Scout was most concerned as he considered Polack a blood-brother and watched out for him from day one. A full-blooded Cherokee Indian, Scout bonded with Polack during his first night in the bush. When Scout woke Polack for his watch, the Cherry thought he was blind and could not see in the pitch-black darkness of the jungle. Scout led him to the guard position, staying with him for a part of his watch until Polack regained his night vision and was more comfortable. Since then, Scout was instrumental in helping Polack learn the ropes.

The Indian had high cheekbones and a pointed nose which accentuated his tanned and slender face, jet black hair hung over his forehead and ears. He wore an authentic Indian ancestral headband which complimented the beads he wore around his neck. Scout carried pictures in his wallet showing him in full Native regalia back home in South Carolina. Except for the long flowing black hair, anyone could recognize him in the photo. Scout and Frenchie alternated walking point for the squad.

Wild Bill saw that Polack was in a defensive posture and prepared to intercede if this discussion got out of hand. After all, 28 armed men participating in a heated discussion could become deadly.

Wild Bill was a cowboy from El Paso, TX. He carried a photo in his wallet showing him dressed in a bronco buster outfit standing next to a tall trophy for winning one of his many rodeo competitions. Even with his long hair and beard, the face was unmistakably his. Wild Bill's real name was Bill Hickock.

Frenchie was a seasoned vet and leader of the First Squad. He carried the M79 grenade launcher and always kept a beehive round - a special shell that fired pellets like a shotgun – chambered in his weapon. Each round resembled an oversized bullet, one and a half inches in diameter and three inches long. Frenchie's special vest held a combination of beehive rounds, high explosive rounds (like grenades), and white phosphorus rounds, 30 in total. He always wore a black beret, a good-luck charm that an uncle sent him from France. Hence, the nickname. Frenchie remained in the background and just did his job.

Doc, an African - American from Philadelphia, was the medic for the platoon. His goal was to study medicine after his tour ended in January. He was extremely skilled at his trade and liked by all. Doc was also the philosopher in the platoon and often shared words of wisdom with the group.

Once, he talked about friendship and camaraderie, stating that squad members, unknowingly, develop a special bond with one another. It was based upon trust and the dependency on each other for moral support and strength. Troops may not see one another after Vietnam, but they would all remember that special bond forever.

Frenchie, Wild Bill and Scout all arrived at the same time and planned to go home in February.

Just then, Sixpack arrived which put an end to the altercation. "Okay, gather around." He waved them in and waited until the 28 members of the platoon surrounded him, like a huddle during a football game. When they were in place, he began the briefing, "As you all know, Polack and LG were almost discovered on LP last night by 20 or more gooks who took a break almost on top of them, and later, might be the same ones responsible for the mortars we received at the firebase. Rock directed an artillery strike on their location and then later blew an ambush which killed nine enemy soldiers."

Rock's squad members received pats on the back and high-fives from fellow soldiers upon hearing the news.

Sixpack continued, "They gathered all the enemy equipment and had to vacate their position and move closer to the firebase. Battalion wants us to first search through the area where the artillery silenced the mortars and then move to where Rock sprung his ambush for a look around. If all goes well, we should be back by early afternoon."

"What about the monkeys?" someone asked, resulting in snickers and guffaws from the rest of the group.

Polack and LG lowered their heads and shook them side to side. "Enough already!" Polack warned angrily.

Sixpack looked to Polack, a serious look upon his face, "Go ahead and tell them what happened, Polack. Then that's the end of it! Understood?" He received acknowledgments from everybody in the huddle when he faced them individually.

Polack cleared his throat, "As Sixpack said, we had about 20 NVA soldiers stop and take a break on the trail right next to our LP. When a couple of them left the column to piss and shit near us, we thought they'd find our claymores and follow the wires back to where we were hiding." The huddle tightened and individuals were more attentive. "It wasn't long after they left that the mortars started falling on the firebase. We could hear them firing and saw the flashes through the jungle. The CP radio operator also warned us to be on the lookout for a spotter who might be directing the mortar crew as all the rounds landed in key locations within the perimeter. So, LG and I were spooked that somebody was wondering around between us and the firebase. When the artillery fired, we could see those flashes and the fires that started afterwards. Later when Rock sprung his ambush, we had rounds zip by overhead. Luckily, we were huddled in a slight depression or we'd a been toast." LG nodded and grunted in affirmation periodically as if he were responding to a preacher during a church service. "Now after all that, we both heard twigs snapping and brush moving to our front and were about to fire our claymore, when something came flying through the jungle and landed next to us with a thud. The first thing that came to mind was that it was the spotter who tossed a grenade after seeing us. As we jumped out of our hide, I managed to launch a grenade toward the rustling bushes. Mine went off, but the incoming grenade was a dud. Then a few minutes later, it happened a second time, but this time, it was thrown to the opposite side. We both threw a grenade to our front and jumped in the opposite direction. It, too, was a dud. Finally, after the third dud landed, we got back into the hide and blew one of the Claymores. That's when we heard the screeching coming from the jungle. It just so happened that the Colonel was on the horn with us for a sit-rep, and between him and Rock, both determined that our gooks were instead rock apes." Polack scanned the surrounding faces. Nobody was smiling. "So, there you have it. Would you have done anything different?"

Scout and Wild Bill were the first to comment. "You did the right thing, Polack."

"That's some heavy shit!"

"I'm hip."

"That's not the way we heard it this morning. But don't sweat it!"

"First I heard of something like that happening," Frenchie said.

"Did you check out the duds?" Rock asked.

"Naw, it was too dark," LG answered.

"We have to pass the hide on the way out. Maybe we can stop a minute and check it out," Polack suggested.

"Might can do," Sixpack remarked.

Most of the soldiers were curious themselves and wanted to see exactly what was thrown at their two platoon brothers. Conversations ceased and no one made anymore comments. "Okay guys, you got it right from the horse's mouth. So that's the end of it," Sixpack emphasized. "Line it up for an equipment check!"

The group circled around and slapped palms with LG and Polack before moving into a formation for the final inspection before leaving the firebase.

Sixpack walked along the first row of the four-row formation and checked to ensure that everyone carried what they needed. They were all decked out the same except for a few; the grenadiers, radio operators and machine gunners all carried extra weight due to their special equipment. Doc carried his med-bag, the strap draped across a shoulder and supporting the 25 pounds of medical supplies. When he got to LG, he paused for a moment. "What's with the boony hat, LG?"

"Don't ask, sarge."

Shaking his head, Sixpack walked away and continued his assessment of the remaining three squads.

Except for Rock's ambush squad the night before, other members of the First Platoon had not gone beyond the wire, having spent the week working to build the firebase during the day. Blisters broke and callouses already formed.

During that same week, they were also tagged for perimeter bunker guard twice.

Grunts get antsy about staying in the same place and doing the same thing day in and day out. Longing for the bush, they were excited and gung-ho to go out on this patrol.

"Lock and load!"

The soldiers pulled back charging handles on the weapons and released them. The spring activated cylinder loaded a single round from the magazine and drove it into the firing chamber with a loud metallic clang. All weapons were now hot.

"Move out!" Sixpack ordered.

Chapter Two

Firebase Lynch stood on a patch of land southeast of the city of Tay Ninh and within the footprint of an area identified as the Iron Triangle. Three lines drawn on a map outlined the 125 square miles of thick forests and rubber trees. The three points of the triangle connected the towns of Ben Cat, Ben Suc, and Phu Hoa. The Boi Loi and Hobo Woods bordered the Triangle along one side and the Fil Hol and Michelin Rubber Plantations on the other. The Iron Triangle was known to be an enemy stronghold, filled with miles of tunnels, underground hospitals, training centers, base camps and rest points dating back to before World War II; a troubled area for many years.

In the early part of the war, American and Army of the Republic of Vietnam (ARVN) forces destroyed most of the villages in the Triangle and relocated those families to new facilities in a different area of the country. Much of the Triangle then became a "free fire zone", meaning curfews did not apply, and anyone out and about was considered the enemy. Soldiers were expected to shoot first without requiring clearance. Those remaining villages on the outskirts of the Triangle were extremely supportive of both the Viet Cong (VC) and North Vietnamese Army (NVA) troops, making the fight to drive out the enemy almost impossible. The Triangle was always a major gateway between the infamous Ho Chi Minh Trail in Cambodia, and Saigon, the capital of South Vietnam.

However, a large portion of the jungle within the Triangle provided concealment for hundreds of active infiltration routes. The U.S. Army deemed it necessary to build a firebase right in the middle of Indian country and inserted the First Battalion 27th Infantry (Wolfhounds) of the 25th Infantry Division into this quagmire to stop the flow of fresh enemy troops and supplies.

Rock and his squad led the platoon through the gate, leaving the relative safety of the firebase behind. Once outside, the platoon split in half and morphed into two columns approximately 30 feet apart. Rock and his men continued along on the right and were followed by Fourth Squad. Frenchie assumed point for the First Squad on the left, and Third Squad followed, bringing up the rear of that column.

The engineers used Rome Plows to push back the jungle 200 meters beyond the wire, providing those bunker guards on the perimeter an unobstructed view and open fields of fire in the event of enemy ground attacks. However, last night's rain created puddles and made the clay slick as ice. The ground was uneven and covered with large, deep tracks from the heavy equipment. Exposed tree roots, pieces of tree bark, branches and bowling ball-sized chunks of clay added to the obstacle course. Soldiers performed rare ballet steps as they tiptoed, teetered and pirouetted across the bulldozed landscape. During this portion of the trek, a few soldiers lost their balance and slid through the red mud; two fell and were immediately covered in slime. Those behind helped them up and then continued as if nothing happened. Miraculously, nobody twisted an ankle or got hurt during the short hump through the wasteland.

Once they entered the lush jungle, the footing became stable, but the ground damp and spongy, felt like walking on a trampoline. The light disappeared in the triple canopy, looking more like dusk instead of late morning.

The damp ground and musty smell made Polack uncomfortable. When he looked back into the clearing, the bright sunlight affected his eyes as it did when exiting a dark movie theater in the middle of the day.

Neither column followed the earlier path into the jungle in fear of booby traps and ambushes. Instead, each cut its way through the thick jungle. 'Wait-a-minute vines' were plentiful, (vines with long thorns that snagged packs and shirts causing one to abruptly stop and back up to disengage) but without full packs on their backs, the soldiers easily maneuvered through them.

After hacking through the vegetation for 30 minutes, Rock stopped the column and called for Sixpack to come forward. "Check out this fresh trail," he said, pointing to the right where a pathway cut through the jungle and ended at the main hardpacked trail between the two columns about 20 feet away. It looked like a tunnel in the jungle, clear enough for a file of soldiers to walk through.

Sgt. Holmes and LG followed it and exited onto the hard-packed trail that both the ambush team and enemy soldiers followed yesterday.

"That must be the path cut by the gooks we heard last night," LG volunteered. "Yeah, and here's where they stopped for their break." He lifted a fish tin into the air from the end of a stick.

Sixpack sniffed at the empty container. "Smells like sardines."

Just then, a slight rustle sounded in the jungle to their right as Sgt. Rock, his RTO (Radio Telephone Operator), and the rest of his squad exited from the new trail. "This wasn't here yesterday," he commented.

"Yeah, LG says that's where the gooks came from last night and chowed down right where you're standing."

A few of the soldiers scoured the area to see if the enemy dropped anything of value during their break.

Polack stood watch on the hard-packed trail, his machine gun held at hip level, and pointed north up the trail. BJ and the rest of the column lined up on Polack and dropped in place to provide security along the northern portion of their small perimeter. He soon noticed that this was near the spot where he and LG hid in the underbrush on LP. The depression, a mere 20 feet above the trail, was still filled with water and surrounded by thick brush.

"Hey, Polack," Sixpack beckoned.

He turned around.

"Come here," Sixpack motioned with his head pantomiming for him to join them when their eyes met.

Polack exchanged weapons with BJ, trading the M-60 for his M-16 and walked the 30 feet to where the two sergeants stood.

"This where your Claymore detonated, Polack?" Rock asked pointing to the east side of the trail.

A small crater touched the edge of the four-foot wide hard packed trail, the foliage on the other side literally blown bare for about 20 feet. Beyond, quarter-sized holes perforated the hanging banana leaves and pockmarked the thicker trees from the many small projectiles that blew outward when the mine was triggered.

"Yeah, that's it."

Rock and his RTO then left the small group and continued up the northern trail, passing through the temporary perimeter to look for signs of the enemy.

Sixpack walked into the kill zone and dragged his foot through the black dirt where he saw three other depressions that looked like tiny foxholes. "Your grenades must have landed here," he stated matter of factly. LG and Polack glanced over the area and just nodded their heads in response.

Sixpack turned to the soldiers, "Why don't you both take a look around for those dud grenades."

"Will do." Polack pulled LG by the arm in passing and led him toward their former hide.

Meanwhile Sixpack left the area and joined Rock on the northern trail, where they followed it for about 30 meters.

"Odd that such a well-used trail runs across the entire eastern portion of the firebase?"

"And less than a half a click away from the perimeter."

"Yeah, but this trail's been here long before we arrived." Sixpack used his towel to wipe the sweat from his face and neck.

"Got to lead somewhere."

"I agree with you there, Rock, but that's a patrol for another day."

When the threesome returned to the junction in the trail, LG and Polack joined them a moment later. "No sign of grenades, but we found these rocks," both held large-sized stones in their hands. "These stood out like a sore thumb on the ground with nothing else coming close." Four rocks in the shape of large Idaho potatoes weighed over a pound each.

Rock took one and hefted it in his hand. "These bad boys would have knocked your ass silly if they hit either of you on your head."

"Would have caused some major pain if they hit you anywhere else," Bert, Rock's RTO, added while eyeing the prehistoric weapons.

"Heavy little buggers, too," Sixpack said. "I could see how they'd sound like a grenade if landing nearby in the pitch black of night."

Polack and LG both smiled.

Some of the nearby soldiers scanned the treetops hoping to spot the family of rock apes that attacked the LP, probably more concerned about falling rocks than the monkeys.

The other soldiers returned empty handed from their search of the enemy break area.

"Okay, line 'em up, we move out in two minutes."

Sgt. Rock and his RTO returned with their squad through the same tunnel they exited earlier. Everyone else left their perimeter positions and joined back up in a column formation, 20 feet to the side of the eastbound trail.

The two columns started moving again through the dense vegetation, wary not only of enemy soldiers, but now of apes tossing rocks from above.

When they arrived at Rock's ambush location, there was no question that a firefight took place here; brass casings from weapons of both sides littered the trail, glistening in the small open area like dropped gems on this narrow, bloody path. The dead enemy soldiers were gone!

Just like at the LP, the foliage across the trail was flattened and blown apart by the exploding Claymore mines. But here, the surrounding foliage was covered in blood splatter, pieces of flesh and clothing. Deep red stains where the bodies had bled out saturated the ground.

"Get security out," Sixpack ordered.

Frenchie directed his squad members to their positions. Polack and BJ set up farther east beyond the ambush site and positioned the M-60 to cover the trail that continued eastward. Wild Bill, Scout, Nung, and Doc settled in next and covered the rest of that quadrant until they faced due north. Frenchie positioned himself 10 feet beyond Doc, aiming his M-79 Grenade Launcher toward the jungle beyond the Claymore blast area.

Third Squad set up and covered the quadrant from Frenchie to the west, facing the way they came, while Second and Fourth Squads mirrored the defenses on the southern portion of the perimeter beyond the ambush site.

LG shadowed Sixpack with the radio as Rock explained the previous night's events.

"Our squad was positioned behind that dropped tree beyond the trail," Rock pointed to the south side of the trail.

"A great spot for an ambush," Sixpack agreed.

"We set out mechanicals on both ends of the trail, expecting the gooks that Polack informed us about, to come from their direction up the trail. Then, as a safety, we put another about 50 feet into the jungle to our front expecting them to exit that way after being caught in the ambush."

Sixpack, LG, Rock and Bert spread out and walked through the kill zone for several minutes before returning to the center of their perimeter.

"There's drag marks and blood trails leading away along the east trail," Rock said.

"Yeah, we saw blood splotches on the foliage leading through the jungle and heading in the same direction," Sixpack added.

"Interesting. I wonder if there are some shallow graves nearby. We know for certain there were no survivors."

"How many bodies did you say you counted, Rock?"

"There were at least nine as that's how many weapons we recovered. There were mostly intact bodies, but some body parts were scattered about, too."

"Where did the bodies go?" Bert asked.

Sixpack looked at the short, disheveled RTO with red hair and freckles. "Most Vietnamese are Buddhists and believe that if their body is not buried then the soul wanders around for eternity. Most of the time, if there's survivors, they'll come back and police up the bodies. So, when we come back later, we'll look around for those graves."

Bert shook his head in understanding. "Makes sense."

"I didn't know that shit," LG commented.

"We spotted some blood on the fallen tree that you all used for cover. Was that from your guys, Rock?"

"Yeah, we had to medivac two before moving out to our new location."

"Hurt bad?"

"I heard from Top just before leaving this morning that both would be okay and would probably rest up in Cu Chi and be back in a few weeks."

"That's good news." Sixpack referenced his map, "Where did the mortars fire from?"

"Due north about half a click," Rock pointed to the jungle beyond the blast area.

"Okay, we'll come back and check out that eastern trail after reconning this other area. Get your guys together and we'll leave when you get here."

Rock and Bert disappeared through the foliage to where the other two squads were pulling security.

Sixpack lit a cigarette, then spoke on the radio to let battalion know what they found and that the platoon would leave shortly for their next objective.

Even from 50 feet, Polack made out the noticeable jagged scar on Sgt. Holmes' face. It started just above his top lip, a thick black mustache concealing most of it. then continued across the left side of his face, ending abruptly below the ear. Polack knew that it was the result of a car accident 12 years earlier, one that claimed the life of his older brother.

It was no secret that Sgt. Holmes was a former Drill Sergeant at Fort Polk, and that Polack, Larry, and a couple others in the Third Platoon had trained with him. Having spent a year in Vietnam with the First Cav in 1968, he volunteered for another tour shortly after AIT graduation in

July, citing harassment by the civilians while on leave. He arrived a week before his former students, and now as the First Platoon Sergeant, he was responsible for a couple of them once again. Small world! Sixpack got his nickname after being seen locking a 6-pack of beer in his duffel bag as a good luck talisman prior to coming out to the field. He planned to drink it on the way back home at the end of his tour. The duffel was locked securely in the company supply storage hut back in Cu Chi.

Ten minutes later, the platoon was on the move again. Rock and Frenchie once again led their individual columns through the dense jungle.

As the patrol continued north, the jungle surrounding them became withered and sparse.

"What happened to this part of the jungle?" Polack asked. "It looks like somebody sprayed weed killer all over it."

"It is a weed killer," Sixpack replied. "Special planes used to fly all through this country to spray defoliant on the jungle."

"Why did they spray the countryside?"

"To eliminate and uncover all the enemy hiding places. They had names for the operation and for the shit they sprayed, but I can't remember either of them. Hell, during my last tour, I can even remember them spraying while we were patrolling through the jungle below. The shit came down like a monsoon rain and smelled terrible. We used to get skin rashes that itched like hell and breathing problems from inhaling the stuff."

"Was it dangerous?"

"Other than the rashes and stuff, everybody told us the stuff isn't dangerous and not to worry about it."

"This area smells like shit, too!" Scout added.

"Must be the decomposition," Doc reported.

"Dead bodies have smelled better."

All the porous tree stumps were havens for red ants, spiders, horseflies, and other crawling insects, which feasted on the rotting vegetation. Most of the men were preoccupied with taking defensive measures against the small insects instead of focusing on the patrol. Red ants stung unmercifully; horseflies left welts after biting their victims, and hundreds of spiders sent chills down the spines of the young men.

Chapter Three

When reaching the area where the artillery barrage had hit, damage was widespread and devastating. It looked like a tornado passed through this area; shredded parts of the former jungle piled high in spots and made it difficult for the men to move through the area. Frenchie came upon a single crater larger than the rest, looking as if a much more powerful explosion had created it. The ground and surrounding area, blackened and bare of vegetation, burned out completely for twenty feet around.

"Look at all this shit!" Frenchie turned slowly, taking in the immediate area.

Sixpack and Rock joined Frenchie at the head of the column, while Polack and BJ stood only a few feet away, looking on in awe.

"Did you hear a secondary explosion last night?"

"Nope," Rock responded.

"What about the two of you?" Sixpack looked to LG and then Polack.

"Not me."

LG shook his head.

"It sure looks like one of the 105 rounds landed in a pile of their mortar rounds, the explosion must have annihilated the mortar crew."

Two squads were dispatched to sweep through the area and beyond to see what they could find.

The 12 small artillery craters were confined to a 100 foot by 100 foot area. Fresh, black dirt coated the red ground and nearby vegetation. There were no trees in this open area, but the hot steel projectiles shredded much of the foliage surrounding each crater. The grunts collected several pieces of jagged steel, no larger than a Zippo lighter, as souvenirs.

"Man, if there was somebody out here last night, you'd think there was no way they could have survived. Just look at all this. It's fucked up!" Polack said, sweeping his arm in a half-circle arc.

"Yeah, but keep in mind that at least nine survivors made it to Rock's ambush site," Wild Bill said while pocketing a jagged piece of shrapnel as thick as a finger but an inch longer.

"I'm sure some survived the ambush and returned to collect the dead," Scout added.

"I wouldn't be surprised if there was a basecamp around here, Scout, with additional soldiers."

"Hard to say, Frenchie. If not, the bodies were all vaporized."

"Always a possibility."

"Guys, I found something," Polack announced.

The men rushed over to see what he found. BJ was the first to arrive, "That's so gross! What do you make of it, Doc?"

"I need a closer look." Doc moved forward, swinging his arms wildly to bat away swarms of flies that had gathered on that portion of the tree. "It's definitely human bone and tissue. There's more over here!" He pointed out several smaller pieces with black hair strewn about the area. "The largest piece I can see is about as big as a Zippo lighter."

"Vaporized it is!" Scout announced.

Upon closer investigation, they found more pieces of human flesh clinging to foliage and littering the ground at the far end of the western perimeter.

Nung had wandered out beyond the devastation to snoop around. A former VC soldier, he surrendered to the south, completed re-education, and then volunteered to be a scout for the Americans. He stood about five feet tall and probably weighed 80 pounds. As a member of the Wolfhounds for about three years, Nung primarily worked with the First Platoon and had saved their asses several times. His English was half-assed, but he proved himself as a scout, skilled interpreter and interrogator. Nobody had a reason not to trust him. Other units had experiences where their Kit Carson Scout either gave them up or disappeared in the bush only to rejoin their former units. In Nung's case, he had a score to settle because the VC massacred his family after he surrendered. On one occasion, he picked up a discarded AK-47 and emptied an entire magazine into the head of a dead VC soldier after a firefight.

Plenty of dead wood lay about, some still smoldering from fires created by the artillery barrage less than 12 hours earlier.

Polack saddled up to LG, "Remember last night, the flickering and glowing flames looked like small campfires grouped together?"

"Yeah, I'm hip. They kept burning all night and I thought we might have us a forest fire."

"Never happen, the foliage was moist to begin with and then the rain started."

"Yeah, but the shit is still burning as we speak."

Suddenly, Nung trotted back to where Sixpack and others were looking through the area. He carried something excitingly in his hand. "Sargin Home, look what Nung find."

He handed Sixpack what looked like a corner portion of an olive drab colored metal box. On top, red Russian letters surrounded two dials and a toggle switch, an antenna mount was in the corner, but nothing was attached. A four-inch piece of green jagged steel ran along one side which was all that remained from the housing. Brown stains covered the piece.

"Fuckers had a radio," Sixpack exclaimed.

"That's what the CP told us last night while we were on the LP. The RTO informed us that they might have a spotter and to keep alert," Polack informed the group.

"Had to be," Sixpack said while inspecting the piece of hardware. "The mortar rounds landed too perfectly inside the perimeter. One or two more and they would have had direct hits on the Command Bunker." He then handed the remnant to Rock.

"I wonder where that spotter di-di'd (slang for ran off) to after he lost contact?" LG asked.

"This is fucked up. That gook might have been the one who got too close and tripped the flares out on the perimeter last night." Polack added.

"Fer sure, he knew not to come your way since you and the monkeys were already duking it out," Frenchie quipped.

This brought snickers from those standing nearby. Even Polack and LG laughed.

"So how many KIA you figure at this location?"

"Five," Rock surmised.

"Why five?" Sixpack asked.

"Crew of three, the radio operator, and an ammo bearer."

"Anybody find blood trails leading away from here?" Sixpack called out.

Heads shook negatively from those scouring the perimeter.

"I think most of them di-di'd toward us once the artillery began, and those staying behind were all killed when a round hit their ammunition cache," Rock said.

"Okay, nine plus five equals fourteen. So, if this was the same group that Polack and LG estimated at twenty, then six of them got away."

"Or more," Rock added while examining what was left of the Russian radio housing.

Sixpack got on the horn to give a sit-rep to the CP and then informed them that after a break, they would make their way back to the ambush site to recon the eastern trail beyond that point. The drag marks and blood trails leading that way piqued everyone's curiosity.

"Okay, take a break. We leave in thirty minutes," Sixpack announced.

Most, if not every soldier brought along C-Rations in their trouser pockets, knowing full well that patrols usually lasted longer than just a couple of hours. It was already noon and they had been outside of the firebase for three hours already.

Nobody brought stoves or heat tabs with them understanding that whatever they brought would have to be eaten cold.

"What you got, Polack?" Scout asked.

"Scrambled eggs," he said between mouthfuls.

"Not a bad choice. I'm a fan of cold beans and weenies myself," Scout ran a P-38 opener around the rim of a can.

"Spaghetti and meatballs is good cold, too," BJ added.

"I've got pound cake and peaches," Wild Bill boasted. This elicited moans from the group as that combination was one of the most sought-after desserts in the bush.

Doc smiled and held up a can in each hand, "Applesauce and a pecan roll."

"Trade?" a couple soldiers chimed in.

Doc shook his head and smiled in satisfaction.

Nung was munching on a rice ball and taking bites from a dried fish wrapped in paper. He still had access to his local village and got passes to visit whenever the platoon was at the basecamp. He would not eat C-Rations and refilled his stash whenever an opportunity presented itself.

"What did you eat?" Doc asked Frenchie, who had just finished digging a hole. He tossed two cans in and then brushed dirt to cover them. "Crackers and peanut butter," he said, before taking two long pulls from his canteen.

Some of the soldiers leaned against trees or lay flat on the ground to catch a few minutes of sleep to recharge. Wiped out from the sleepless night, Rock's ambush squad had not slept since 2200 hours the night before when the LP warned about the enemy soldiers heading their way. The rest of the platoon members manned the perimeter bunkers and stayed awake after the mortar attack on the firebase. Fortunately, soldiers had learned over time to grab a few winks whenever possible as no guarantee existed when the next opportunity would come.

Sixpack walked through the area of prone soldiers, "Everybody up and back in formation," he prompted. "Call in the OP's and get ready to move out! We're going back to the ambush site, same order of march. We leave in three minutes."

Chapter Four

Sixpack split the platoon into two sections: two squads followed the drag marks and blood trails on the eastward hard pack, and the other two followed blood splatters on foliage leading away from the kill zone. Both groups would continue eastward and meet at the blue line (stream) shown to be about two clicks away.

Scout and Frenchie shared the point and cut through the jungle following the broken brush and blood splotches. They witnessed multiple Ho Chi Minh sandal footprints in the soft dirt alongside the drag marks, some crisscrossing over the another.

"Looks like two of them are dragging the bodies," Scout pointed to the prints and drag marks overlapped along the path.

"You keep watching the ground and I'll keep an eye on our front," Frenchie used his M-79 to push aside long drooping vines, banana leaves, and clumps of vegetation that hung from the overhead canopy.

Nung, BJ, Polack, Doc, and Wild Bill kept about 20 feet behind the two point men; Third Squad followed behind them. Everyone's head was on a swivel looking through the surrounding jungle and treetops. Sixpack and LG positioned themselves three-quarters of the way back in the column, near the middle of the Third Squad.

Sgt. Rock had split his group in two so a squad could move on each side of the six-foot wide path, hard packed with plenty of overhead clearance, yet camouflaged by the overhead canopy and unseen from the air.

They followed the blood splatter and drag marks for about 50 meters before they disappeared. Soon they came upon wagon wheel depressions in the dirt along with fresh boot prints among the many Ho Chi Minh sandal prints.

Rock ordered a halt and called Sixpack on the radio. "Sierra-One-Six this is Sierra-Three-Six."

"Go, Three," Sixpack responded.

"Roger, be advised that our blood trails ended not far from the ambush site and we've come across wagon wheel depressions on the trail along with boot and sandal prints."

"This is One-Six, how many prints?"

"Lots."

"Roger, Three. Proceed with caution. We'll continue tracking through this area and see where it leads us."

"Wilco, out."

Sgt. Rock sent out flankers 25 feet to the side of each column to help with the security as they continued following the wagon wheel tracks.

The afternoon heat took its toll on the warriors as they continued through the jungle. Their shirts already saturated with sweat, green flashes occurred periodically as soldiers used their green towels to wipe sweat from heads and faces.

Canteens also magically appeared and disappeared along the columns.

Suddenly, Scout and Frenchie took a knee and raised a fist into the air. This stopped their column, and those following behind quickly dropped to a knee.

"Sixpack, up," the request relayed and whispered from one man to the next down the line until it reached Sgt. Holmes.

"Come on, LG." Both soldiers rose, hunched over and headed to the front of the column.

Frenchie waved them lower to the ground and held a finger across his lips, signaling them to be quiet in their movements.

"What's up, guys?" Sixpack whispered.

"Got movement to our right. We keep hearing sounds in that direction."

Sixpack took out his compass and noticed that the column was now moving in more of a southeast direction instead of true east like they began. "It could be the rest of the platoon out on the trail."

Sixpack grabbed the handset from LG. "Sierra-Three-Six this is Sierra-One-Six."

"Go ahead, One."

"Have your men stop in place. We've got movement to our right and we're not sure if it's gooks or you guys. I'm sending Scout and Nung to check it out."

"Roger, standing by."

Nung took the lead as he and Scout duckwalked and crawled through the thick foliage toward the source of the noise. Both were stealthy in their movements and overly cautious as they proceeded in that direction.

Rock's left flank soldier faced north on his knees, away from the rest of the squad members on the trail. He heard nothing nearby and wiped his face with a towel when Scout and Nung jumped up a few feet away. The surprise caused him to lose his balance and fall backwards. "Jesus, you scared the fuck out of me," the surprised flanker remarked after a shocking moment.

"Just think if we were gooks. You'd a been dead by now," Scout chastised the Cherry. Nung smiled and ran his finger across his throat showing that he could have quietly disposed of the man.

"Stay right here until Rock tells you to move again. And get your shit together, troop, you may not be so lucky next time!"

The two men returned to Sixpack and informed him of their find.

"Sierra-Three-Six this is Sierra-One-Six."

"This is Sierra-Three-Six."

"Roger, proceed up the trail, our direction of movement looks like we're heading toward the trail and should hook-up with you in a short. Also, send some toilet paper out to your flanker, he might need to clean up."

"Roger. Sierra-Three-Six, out." Rock, curious about Sixpack's last comment, walked out to his flanker to find out what happened.

Thirty minutes later, the platoon was whole again and joined up on the trail. Here, the wheel indentations sank deeper into the dirt indicating that the weight of the load had increased.

"Looks like all the dead soldiers were put on the cart and moved further down this trail."

"Yeah, Sixpack, and it looks like a lot of gooks are with them," Rock stated, pointing out the footprints in the dirt.

"Take five, I've got some calls to make."

The platoon members sat in place, but the knowledge of the cart and lots of enemy soldiers increased their sense of vulnerability.

"Thunder-Three this is Sierra-One-Six, over."

"This is Thunder-Three go ahead."

"Sierra-One-Six, we've followed blood trails to the east beyond the ambush site about a click and have come across heavy traffic and cartwheel tracks on the hard pack. Estimate we're still about a click away from the blue line."

"Any enemy bodies?"

"Negative. But we think the cart was used to transport them."

"Roger. What's your current location?"

"Wait one." Sixpack marked the estimated location on his map and gave the coordinates to LG so he could cypher them. When he finished, he handed a scratch pad to Sixpack.

"Thunder-Three, Sierra-One-Six, over."

"Thunder-Three, go ahead with coordinates."

"This is Sierra-One-Six. Roger, I shackle Romeo – Romeo – Alpha – Foxtrot – Echo – November."

"Roger. Good copy. Wait one for Bulldog-One."

Bulldog-One was the battalion commander, Colonel Jonathan Smith.

"Sierra-One-Six, Bulldog-One, over."

"This is Sierra-One-Six, go ahead Bulldog."

"I have your location not far from the blue line. Continue following the trail to see whether or not it leads to the blue line."

"Wilco Bulldog-One, Sierra-One-Six, out."

Sixpack gathered the troops together and rolled out his plan. "We'll continue to follow this trail and see where it leads. We're only about a click away from the stream so we'll figure things out when we get there. Shouldn't take us long. And if all goes well, we could still be back in time for dinner."

"It's already 1430 hours and we're four clicks from the firebase."

"I know, Wild Bill. Let's see how it all plays out."

The patrol continued its trek toward the river without any mishaps. Everything seemed normal; the jungle was alive with chirps, screeches, croaks, and the rustling sounds of the wind blowing through the overhead foliage. A slight rushing sound could be heard in the near distance, but before they had an opportunity to investigate, Scout and Frenchie called for another halt. "Sixpack, up," the request passed back from man to man.

When he and LG arrived, they had no need to ask what was up. Sixpack saw for himself that the cartwheel tracks had turned off the trail and now headed toward a small area cleared of shrubbery. Nung migrated to the front of the column so as not to miss out on anything.

"You three follow the tracks into the cleared area and see where they go," Sixpack said.

Nung, Scout, and Frenchie proceeded through the brush and into the cleared area, ground devoid of any foliage for almost 20 yards squared. The thick overhead canopy still prevented sunshine from penetrating to the floor of the jungle. The tracks turned abruptly in the clearing and headed west. Nung continued to follow the ruts while Scout moved across to the other side and Frenchie turned right to follow the tree line.

A shrill whistle stopped the men in the clearing. It came from Nung, waving his arms excitedly. Frenchie and Scout hurried over to his position. Nestled along the edge of the clearing they counted 17 shallow graves; nine were fresh. A small Buddha figurine sat on a makeshift miniature altar next to a sand filled glass bowl holding burnt incense sticks. Thankfully, none were lit. It sat closer to the corner of the area in between the graves and where the shrubbery began.

"We find graves," Nung proudly announced.

"Yeah, but why carry the bodies all this way?" Frenchie thought out loud. "It doesn't make sense."

"Must be a tribal cemetery," Scout announced. "There's eight more graves that look like they've been here a while and these fresh ones just continued where the others ended."

"VC cemetery here mean beaucoup danger for GI." Nung said. "Camp maybe not far."

"You know this for sure?"

"Not for sure, but if VC camp stay long time then have cemetery same same."

"I'll head back and get Sixpack." With that Frenchie turned and jogged back to the opening they came through.

Several minutes later, the rest of the platoon entered the clearing. Sixpack pointed where he wanted the squads to set up around the clearing to provide security while they investigated the graveyard. Squads of soldiers peeled off from the column and headed in different directions to encircle the clearing.

Frenchie, Sixpack, LG, and Rock arrived at the graves.

"Now, this is interesting," Sixpack said as they walked along the graves. An earthy smell in the air mixed with the smell of sour milk and garbage, a slight hint of incense also remained.

"You want to dig them up?" Rock asked.

"I'm not sure. I know the gooks have used shallow graves to hide caches of weapons and other supplies, but they've always been found in odd places. This is too organized. And the Joss sticks make it seem like there was a ceremony or friends coming to visit."

"Out here?" Frenchie asked. "I've never seen anything like this."

"Many grave all together one place mean beaucoup VC camp not far. Dey here long time and grave from same same soldier who live camp."

"You think the dead from Rock's ambush were from this camp?"

"Aye, Sargin Home. New GI firebay make VC angry," Nung pointed back toward Firebase Lynch.

"Makes sense," Sixpack began. "Most basecamps and bunker complexes that I've come across were near streams. Let me see what battalion wants to do."

Sixpack and LG walked to the center and called Bulldog-One on LG's radio. During the conversation, he removed his map and referenced it, then repeatedly checked his watch. LG watched as the Sgt. became animated and raised his voice a few times. Embarrassed, he turned away from the sergeant.

"It don't look good," Scout mentioned as he watched the conversation unfold.

"We're gonna get fucked over again. Just watch!" Wild Bill said.

Sgt. Rock did not say a word. He and his exhausted squad members hoped to return to the firebase soon. Sgt. Rodriguez, nicknamed Rock, was a Hispanic from New Mexico with a chiseled physique, tan complexion, and jet-black hair. An avid weightlifter, he created a makeshift set of barbells and dumbbells at the firebase from pipe and cement filled paint cans on the ends. Other soldiers envied his square chin, tight facial features and sixpack abs. He reminded many of the Sgt. Rock comic book character so the nickname stuck.

Sixpack returned with a disgusted look on his face. "Rock, get some men to dig up a couple of these graves. Higher up wants us to be certain that they aren't caches."

Rock's face showed surprise but he composed himself before walking back to his people.

Wild Bill came over from his position only a few yards away. "What's the deal, Sixpack?"

"Digging up some graves."

"Why? We're not gonna find anything except the remains of some dead gooks."

"Stow it, Wild Bill. We do as we are told."

Polack and BJ continued to watch the jungle to their front but turned around occasionally to watch the goings on near the graves.

"Looks like Sixpack and Wild Bill are arguing again."

"Sure don't look like any of them's happy."

Several minutes later, Rock returned with a couple of soldiers in tow, both carrying fold-up shovels. "Pick a couple and see what you find," he suggested.

The two men detailed for grave digging took out cigarettes, broke off the filters, and stuck them up their noses to help diminish the smell they would soon encounter. The first grave they chose was a new one at the very end of the row. On their knees, both used entrenching tools to scoop away the dirt from on top and pull the dark soil toward them. Removing only a few inches of dirt exposed the black pajama like uniform used by VC soldiers. Dropping their shovels, they used both hands to scoop away the remaining dirt. The stench of death escaped into the air making some of those nearby soldiers gag. Before long, they uncovered the body and ensured nothing else remained under the dirt. Nung stood a short distance away with his hands folded, forefingers touching and pointing to his front. Anybody would think he was praying.

The contorted body, black pajamas torn and bloody, both hands resting on his chest, and face showed signs of surprise, fear, and pain with a mouth wide open as if calling out for help. Rigor mortis had already set but the lack of vermin signaled that decomposition had not started.

Poking the shovels into the dirt under the body yielded no striking metal or wood. The two soldiers looked up at Sixpack shaking their heads negatively to indicate the absence of a cache.

"Okay, guys, pick one of the others. Wild Bill, you and Scout cover the body back up."

Wild Bill offered a look of disgust before he dropped to his knees and quietly pushed the loose dirt back over the exposed body.

They repeated the same exercise at another grave in the middle of the row with the same results.

When the graves were returned as found, Sixpack gathered the squad leaders together for an update. "The colonel wants us to continue on to the stream and check things out. If we don't find anything, we can head back to the firebase."

The men looked hopeful that the patrol was coming to an end.

"Same order of march. Gather up where we came into the clearing and we'll leave when we're all together."

Five minutes later, the platoon crept along both sides of the trail and moved toward the stream. The sound of rushing water became louder as they neared the blue line.

Surprisingly, the river was approximately 50 feet across, and the water moved rapidly in a moderate northern current. Several large boulders lay haphazardly in the stream, water splashing against them and exploding to the sides. The liquid somewhat clear, unlike most that were brown or dark green colored, still obstructed the view of the bottom. Little sunshine also poked through the overhead canopy and rays penetrated momentarily when an occasional breeze opened spots in the ceiling of tree branches.

"Sixpack, over here." Rock called, motioning from the water's edge near where the trail led into the stream.

"Well kiss my ass," Sixpack acknowledged after realizing what Rock was pointing at.

An underwater bridge constructed of bamboo and twine connected the two shorelines. Six inches of water covered the walkway, unseen unless standing next to it. On the other side of the stream, the hard packed trail split; one continued east and slightly uphill while the other turned left and ran parallel along the river.

"This ain't good, and I'm getting bad vibes about it." Rock said.

"Yeah, let's tell the colonel we didn't find anything and head back to the firebase. It's already 1600 hours and it'll be dark in another two hours."

"Let's see what the man has to say about it, LG." Sixpack held out his arm for the radio handset.

After speaking with the colonel, Sixpack called the men together. "Listen up. The colonel is sending out a platoon from Charlie Company to relieve us and ambush the trail crossing by the river tonight. We're to wait for them and then head back to the firebase. To get here quickly, they're going to use the hard-packed trail. After we link up, we'll take the same trail back to the firebase."

"So, what do we do meanwhile?" one of the squad leaders asked.

"We'll line up along the south side of the trail to wait in the scrub for them. Once they arrive, we'll step out to meet them and head home."

The platoon members moved into the jungle brush on the side of the trail, Frenchie, Scout, and the rest of their squad were positioned on the far right and would be first to see their relief coming. All were content and in a rather good mood knowing the patrol would be moving in less than an hour.

At 1645, sudden explosions and the eruption of gunfire to the west surprised the hunkered down soldiers in the First Platoon. The pop-pop sounds of AK-47's rose in crescendo, predominant in the near distance. After what seemed like minutes later, the sharp crack of M-16's and deep thumping of M-60 machine gun fire and exploding grenades entered the fray. The noise was deafening! RTOs tuned to the battalion frequency, listening intently to the communication taking place.

LG volunteered, "The platoon from Charlie Company was ambushed on the trail approximately a click away; halfway between us and Rock's ambush site last night. Several soldiers are wounded and urgent medivacs are requested."

Sixpack wasted no time and ordered the platoon members to quickly form into an inverted "L" formation to cover the western approach and the trail in the event enemy soldiers broke contact and headed in their direction.

"Anybody got Claymores?" The question ran up and down the line of soldiers. Negative, since this was only to be a short recon mission. Possibly facing an onslaught of VC troops, the soldiers possessed nothing more than firearms and grenades.

The AK-47 fire tapered off and eventually stopped after 15 minutes. The American weapons continued to fire in short bursts, hoping to catch stray enemy soldiers still lurking in the kill zone.

Medivac helicopters soon arrived, accompanied by two Cobra helicopters. The two gunships wasted little time and began their rocket and minigun fire into the jungle to the south of the trail. This would keep the enemy heads down while the Red Cross choppers brought up the wounded with jungle penetrators. It would turn out to be a long and arduous process, as almost half of the platoon had to be evacuated.

After the evacuation, the understaffed Charlie Company platoon got online and conducted a 'mad minute' (safety measure where every soldier fired a couple magazines of ammo into an area to enter) into the ambush area prior to stepping off the trail and sweeping through it for another 50 feet. Hundreds of spent cartridges on the ground marked the only remaining sign of an enemy. They found splotches of blood, but no weapons or bodies. Instead of joining up with Alpha Company, the depleted platoon was ordered to return to the firebase.

Alpha's First Platoon would have to be on its own for the night with nothing more than the soldiers' weapons, ammunition, and water.

At 1830 hours, Sixpack gathered the troops and ordered them to form a tight circular perimeter in the heavy brush about 100 meters south of the trail.

"Buddy up in two-man positions and keep each other warm the best you can. Anybody got extra rations to share?"

All their food and snacks were consumed during their lunch break meaning that no rations were available.

"We'll keep the RTOs in the center of the perimeter and take care of the radio sit-reps during the night. I want 50% alert during the night, and you guys on the perimeter work out your own guard schedule. The enemy is out there. Stay alert!"

Nobody voiced disapproval or made derogatory comments challenging these orders.

"Sarge, do you think that ambush with Charlie Company was meant for us?" a soldier asked in the fast-approaching darkness.

"No doubt about it. The VC knew that the firebase would send somebody out to recon the area after last night's firefight and artillery barrage, so the gooks probably had eyes on us all day long. They know how many we are and not equipped for an overnight stay by what we carried. All they had to do was to pick a spot and wait for us to pass on the way back to the firebase. I don't think they expected another unit to approach from the opposite direction and it caught them by surprise."

Looks of panic and dismay swept through the group of soldiers.

"Hunker down as best you can tonight and at first light, we'll play it safe and cut bush back to the firebase."

Nights in Vietnam got cold as the temperature dropped to the low 60s. Troops used poncho liners to keep warm on these chilly nights, carrying them in personal rucksacks with the rest of their supplies. Unfortunately, their rucksacks were left at the firebase. Soldiers draped their moist green towels across their shoulders and huddled up with a partner, leaning against thick trees when available. Several troops only wore sleeveless t-shirts on this patrol, so they would suffer the most during the chilly night.

Polack fell asleep quickly after his watch and a dream entered his subconscious.

A hand covered his mouth and he heard the soldier whisper, "Gooks." Movement in the jungle about 20 meters away sounded like a group making its way through the dense brush. His body stiffened, adrenaline now coursing through it as he realized they were heading straight for him.

When reaching the trail about 10 feet away, the sound of machetes cutting through the vegetation ceased while stomping feet and scuffling replaced it along the dirt trail. Vietnamese voices whispered up and down the trail as the file of enemy soldiers emptied onto the well-used pathway and then suddenly dropped in place. Cigarettes lit among hushed conversations. The smell of fermented fish filled the air.

Polack's heart beat so hard he was certain that those on the trail could hear it. When two of the soldiers broke away from the trail and headed into the brush near his position, he held his breath. One squatted about 10 feet above his head and proceeded to empty his bowels. The horrendous smell almost caused him to gag. The second soldier walked along another trail to his front and stopped near one of the Claymore mines to urinate, his stream forceful, steady, and splashing against the foliage.

After he finished, the soldier turned to rejoin his group, stumbling as he tripped over the Claymore wire leading back to his position. The enemy soldier bent down to pick up the brown wire, examine it, and call out in a sing-song manner to his fellow soldiers.

When the NVA soldier picked up the wire, he inadvertently pulled the blasting cap from the Claymore mine rendering it useless. Several others joined him with weapons pointed forward as he collected the wire and followed it to where Polack sat frozen with fear. The soldier with the bunched wire in hand had just reached Polack's position, his forward movement stopping immediately when his boot crashed into the sole of Polacks'. 'There was no way I would survive this,' Polack thought.

BJ kicked Polack in the boot once again, harder this time, in hopes of waking him from what seemed to be a nightmare, squirming about and mumbling incoherently.

"Polack, wake up man. You're dreaming." BJ whispered loudly then dropped to his knees and shook the soldier.

Polack's eyes suddenly flashed open, unmoving at first, looking straight up, then darting back and forth, confused and momentarily unsure of his whereabouts. He sat up and looked directly into BJ's eyes, a huge smile erupted seconds later. "Oh man, am I glad to see you," he said in a quivering voice.

"I bet you are. The way you was carrying on, I thought you was having a heart attack."

"What time is it?"

"It's six, and everybody's getting up anyway."

"Thanks, bro. I owe you one."

"Don't mean nothin'."

Chapter Five

The night proved uneventful, and everyone was thankful for the absence of rain and enemy soldiers.

The jungle inhabitants woke, screeched greetings reverberating across the treetops along with clicks, snaps, whistles, and grunts from the animals as they called to neighbors and relatives.

Anxious to get underway, Sixpack called battalion for last minute instructions prior to leaving their night defensive position.

Instead, he received a virtual kick in the teeth. The colonel wanted the platoon to cross the stream and do a quick recon prior to returning to the firebase.

Sixpack complained that his men were worn out, hungry, and sleep deprived. Asking them to poke around in an area with a suspected enemy basecamp was a reckless order.

His arguments fell upon deaf ears. "Do the best you can," the colonel responded.

With nothing to pack, the men were restless and eager to get moving. Sixpack feared a revolt when breaking the news.

He drew the soldiers into a tight circle and sat in the center with LG. "Guys, we're not going in just yet."

"You shittin' me?"

"What?" heads turned sideways to those on either side. Looks of disbelief appeared, shoulders shrugged, eyebrows raised, and lips pressed hard against one another.

"The colonel…"

"Fuck that lifer motherfucker. He plays us like we're toy soldiers on a board game," Wild Bill interrupted.

"Yeah, bring his ass out here and let him do what we have to."

The chatter grew louder as the reality hit them.

"We suffered enough for that cocksucker."

"Let's just head back like we planned."

Sixpack kept quiet and let them vent. It only took a couple minutes before they quieted down.

"Done?" he asked, looking each soldier in the eye for just a split second.

Most evaded his eyes but remained quiet.

Once Sixpack had their full attention, he laid out the plan. "Look, this is what we're going to do. Rock, you'll take two squads and follow the northern trail along the water for about 300 meters. The rest of us will cross the stream over the bridge and follow the east trail for the same distance. If we don't find anything, we'll return here and head back to the firebase."

This brought a smile to many of their faces.

"Questions?"

None.

"Okay, let's move out."

Rock and his group lined up and moved out of their hide, and into the jungle a couple feet off the trail following it alongside the stream. Easy moving, it would not take much time at all to complete the short patrol.

Sixpack's patrol was more difficult as they waded across the river on the underwater bridge. Once across, they used the same strategy of walking in the jungle and staying off the trail. Nung and Scout led the group.

About 100 meters in, the men picked up the scent of burning wood. Nung held up a fist and everyone dropped to a knee. He squatted and tried to move the brush to the front with his rifle to get a less obstructed view. What he saw made him anxious.

Sixpack moved up to the two men, not quite believing what he saw. Several thatched huts stood in a cleared area along with bunkers and fighting trenches.

Nung whispered, "Sargin Home, bunker."

"I see them, Nung."

"Not there, here," he said, pointing to his left.

When Sixpack and Scout both turned in that direction, they stared straight into the firing port of a bunker designed to cover the trail.

"Nobody inside, maybe cook rice."

"Fuck me." Sixpack turned and motioned for the men to back up quickly.

Suddenly, Nung and Scout sprang up and opened fire on three surprised NVA soldiers who stepped out onto the trail from the other side of the bunker, both carrying empty containers most likely to fill at the river. One more moment and they would have tripped right over the prone Americans sprawled out on the ground.

"Go, go, go!" Sixpack yelled, waving everyone back and across the river.

Before they even took a step, the sound of a single AK-47 firing was heard from downstream where Rock and his group waited. Seconds later, additional AK47's and M-16's joined in the clamor. A full-fledged firefight just broke out to the north.

As Sixpack's team retreated, a number of AK-47's from the camp opened up and fired blindly at the fleeing soldiers running down the trail. The team members zigged and zagged toward perceived safety. When they reached the stream, waterspouts erupted around them as bullets impacted into the flowing river.

On the other side, Scout and Frenchie noticed Rock's group high tailing it back up their trail toward them and pointed them out, hollering, "Friendlies! Friendlies!" As hyped as everyone was, they did not want a friendly fire incident.

Once the platoon was together again, they double timed up the main trail and away from the stream, running 200 meters before turning south and charging into the dense jungle. The First Squad led the pack and pushed on until reaching an area with several felled trees that provided ample cover in the event the enemy soldiers pursued them. Miraculously, not one soldier was hit during their evasive action.

"The enemy had to be just as surprised as we were. They're probably making plans to come and find us," Frenchie volunteered.

"Not if I can help it," Sixpack added. He quickly got on the horn and called in a fire mission to the artillery battery on Lynch while Rock and Bert apprised the colonel of their situation. Neither team had a chance to debrief the other, figuring it could wait until completing the artillery mission.

A marker round popped high in the air above the coordinates sent by Sixpack, but the triple canopy jungle prevented him from seeing where it exploded. He instructed LG, Nung, Scout, and Wild Bill to accompany him as he jumped over the tree trunks to move closer to the trail and stream intersection. Once in place, he called for a second round.

They still could not see it above the canopy but guessed by the sound and direction that its distance was good, but too far south and to the right. He made an adjustment, asking for a volley of six high-explosive rounds. The whistling overhead gave them a three-second warning before the rounds exploded loudly to their front, CRUMP – CRUMP – CRUMP… landing just where he expected.

Sixpack made several changes and walked the volleys through the area he thought encompassed the basecamp. While he orchestrated the artillery fire, the four men with him maintained their vigilance of the trails and river in case the enemy tried to escape and head toward them during the bombardment. The staff sergeant ended the fire mission after firing 48 rounds at the enemy complex. Moving the volleys as he did, he confidently felt it brought hurt to the enemy. Not one enemy soldier attempted to withdraw from the complex and head their way, so the five men returned to their temporary encampment.

Once the adrenaline subsided, all relaxed and cheered up emotionally.

"Why didn't they chase us?"

"Who knows?" Sixpack said. "I'm surprised, too, since we wandered into their backyard."

"Maybe they thought there were more of us than them."

"We'll never know that answer."

"So, what did you tell the colonel, Rock?"

Rock coughed to clear his throat and then buried his head into a green towel, wiping off layers of sweat from his face and head before replacing it over his shoulders. "First off," he looked directly at Sixpack, "Bulldog-One asked for you and when I told him you were busy directing the artillery, he was pissed and insisted you call him the moment you finish the fire mission. You gonna call him now?"

"Nope. Hell, let him wait."

This comment seemed to please those within earshot on the small perimeter; many smiled broadly and nodded in support.

Sgt. Holmes leaned back against a tree, shrugged his shoulders, and flexed his neck muscles to work out a kink from his neck. "What exactly did you tell the old man?"

Rock lit a cigarette, sucked in deeply, then exhaled a blue cloud of smoke which floated past Sixpack and quickly absorbed into the air surrounding them. "I told him that we had split up into two groups with the intent of following the two trails for a short distance when both groups were ambushed. I added that we made a hasty retreat to a defensible position and were waiting to see if the enemy was going to attack. Then he asked if we noticed any bodies lying about."

Sixpack, drinking from his canteen, almost choked. He coughed and spit some water onto his lap. "Are you shitting me?" he asked incredulously.

"Nope, swear to God! Didn't even ask if we had any casualties."

"Doesn't surprise me any. You'd think the brass got a bonus for every dead enemy body they reported."

"Sometimes it appears that way."

Once again, those within earshot nodded their agreement with the comment.

"So, fill me in on what happened to you guys out there."

Rock took another pull on his cigarette before responding. "We moved along the trail for about 200 meters and didn't see anything out of the ordinary. No tracks, no more bridges crossing the stream, and no fish traps in the water. Everything looked natural. We had just turned around to head back when we heard the M-16 fire coming from your location. We were ready to double-time back when some rounds were fired at us from across the river. We hit the dirt and returned fire to where we thought the sniper was. Then a few seconds later, several more AK's joined in the fight. We didn't have much cover and needed to vacate the area, so we leapfrogged back and covered each squad's movement until meeting up with you. Thank God, nobody got hit."

Those soldiers sitting around the small perimeter listened intently to the reports.

"Doesn't sound like an ambush; more like a sentry spotting you and sending an alarm after taking a couple of pot shots in your direction. The added guns joined in when they arrived."

"Sounds about right," Rock agreed. "What did you guys see?"

Sixpack pulled out a bag of Redman Chewing Tobacco and placed a chunk in the right rear of his mouth between his cheek and wisdom teeth. He chewed several times and then spit out a gob of brown liquid onto the ground. "Once we crossed the bridge, the trail had a slight incline. We went up about a hundred meters before Scout and Nung called for a halt. When I got up there, I was surprised to see several straw huts, bunkers, fighting trenches, and several cooking fires. The ground was clear of all vegetation and shrubs, and the tree canopy covered everything below. In fact, Nung pointed out that we were laying right in front of a bunker firing port that was supposed to cover the trail we were on. It was so well camouflaged that I didn't even notice it. We were just about to pull back when three NVA soldiers stepped out onto the trail from the front of the bunker with water pails. Scout and Nung reacted quickly and put them down but it also alerted the camp to our presence. That's about the time we heard your firefight begin, and like you, it seemed like several soldiers arrived at varying times to take us under fire. We double timed out of there as fast as we could and met up with your team. I'm surprised they didn't give chase, but I wanted to get some artillery in there before waiting too long."

"You guys lucked out with that bunker."

"Yeah, our shit would have been in the wind."

Sixpack spit more brown juice that splashed in several directions after the thick gob landed on a dried concave leaf on the ground.

"Nung was correct back at the cemetery when he thought a basecamp was probably nearby. Good water source, local cemetery, and everything covered by the overhead canopy. Nothing could be seen from above. What more could they ask for?"

"How many you think are there?"

"It's big. Probably a battalion or more."

"That's 500 or more soldiers!"

"These logs ain't gonna hold up if they come gunnin' for us," a soldier from the Second Squad volunteered.

"Don't sweat it. The cannons had to whittle that bunch down some." Sixpack spat again. "I better call the colonel to fill him in and see what he wants to do next."

Sixpack and LG moved off to the side and filled in the battalion commander. The staff sergeant knew that the news thrilled him to no end and could almost visualize bubbles coming out of the colonel's ears and floating upward.

Five minutes later, Sixpack returned to brief the platoon members.

The soldiers were hyped with the building adrenaline so most were anxious for a fight.

"Gather around," Sixpack called to those soldiers forming the perimeter. They walked and scooted over to form a three-deep huddle. "The colonel wants us to stay put."

"Now he's talking."

"It's get even time!"

None of them complained this time about being hungry and tired.

"As for us, the rest of Alpha Company is on the way to back us up. Additionally, the colonel is dispatching an armored unit to come in from the south along the stream, and two platoons from Charlie Company to come in along the stream from the north."

"What's their ETA?"

"Sometime this afternoon. Once they get here and security is established, we'll sweep through the basecamp and see what we find."

"I hope they're bringing food."

"That's affirm! Meanwhile, keep alert and eyes out for movement around us. Let's do this!"

The huddle disintegrated and soldiers returned to their former positions.

Without supplies, the soldiers could not use the lull in activity to write letters, listen to the radio, eat, make hot cocoa and coffee, or read; they could only watch.

A little over an hour later, Nung appeared from the foliage, arms and pockets filled with goods. Once in the perimeter, he dropped the pile and emptied his pockets where Sixpack and LG sat.

"What the fuck?"

"Chop-chop," Nung pantomimed spooning food into his mouth.

The pile contained several clumps of dandelion weeds with their roots, clumps of purple flowers with roots that looked like skinny potatoes, a couple bunches of small white carrots, a pocketful of berries, and three nine-inch-long scaly fish. Everything was already rinsed and dripping moisture, the tiniest roots emanating from the larger and thicker roots looked like unkept whiskers on an old man's face. "Chop-chop for GI now. Fill stomach till C-Ration come."

Nung cleaned and fileted the fish, cutting them into small, cubed pieces. He popped a couple into his mouth and chewed the raw fish, soliciting groans from those nearby, since sushi was still unpopular in the states. A few men on the perimeter took a chance and accepted a meager portion; others waved Nung away. Nobody threw up, thankfully. Next, he chopped up the dandelions and roots, purple flowers, tan roots, and small white carrots, mixing everything together on two large banana leaves. Nung filled two boony hats and sprinkled some spices over them from a small bottle he carried in his pocket. "Take by hand and eat like sarad," Nung scooped out a handful and filled his mouth. Chewing happily, he walked the line with his creation, again, some passed, but most accepted the heartfelt gesture.

"You know this ain't half bad. The tan stuff tastes like potatoes."

"The purple flowers are sweet."

"I never in my life thought I'd ever eat dandelions."

"The white carrots are crunchy and a little mushy inside, but there's a slight carroty taste."

"At least the rumbling in my stomach stopped."

Nung was content and happy he could help his fellow soldiers.

Sixpack had to ask, "How did you catch the fish, Nung?"

Smiling at the sergeant, "Nung hands very fast, catch slow fish. No sweat!"

LG interrupted, handing Sixpack the radio handset. "Sierra-One-Six this is Viper-Two-Three, over."

"This is Sierra-One-Six, go ahead."

"Roger Sierra-One, we're a flight of two birds with some ordinance to drop. Where do you want it?"

This surprised the men. The colonel must have ordered the air strike to make certain no enemy soldiers would make a last stand when they searched through the complex.

"Viper Two-Three, we just completed a fire mission on the suspected base camp and unable to direct you at this time. Can you see smoke coming through the canopy?"

"Roger, One-Six. Looks like the artillery blew down quite a few trees. We have an open view to some of the target area and will use the smoke to guide us in."

"Thank you, Viper Two-Three. Happy hunting. Sierra-One-Six, out."

Sixpack called out a warning, "Bomb drop on the basecamp. Get down and hide behind something. We're still considered danger close and some of the shrapnel might come this far."

Twenty-eight soldiers scrambled to find the best cover.

They could not see the overhead display and only envisioned what the runs looked like from experience. They heard no whistling before the bombs exploded; only a deep boom causing the ground to shake like an earthquake. The loud jet engines were heard circling overhead, the drone-like sound was accentuated by screaming engines as each bomber climbed out of its dive.

Twenty minutes later, Sixpack heard the callback. "Sierra-One-Six, this is Viper-Two-Three. Ordinance expended and returning to base. Good luck down there! Out!"

Fire engulfed the jungle, thick black plumes of smoke escaping into the air and bleeding through the overhead canopy. The wind also carried the crackle and pop sound of green wood burning. There were no enemy soldiers spotted or secondary explosions heard during either of the barrages.

Now it was hurry up and wait!

Chapter Six

Two hours later, a lone helicopter approached the First Platoon's hide, hovered over them for a short, and then moved toward the enemy base camp. After several passes, it rose to 1,500 feet and lazily circled the area.

"Sierra-One-Six this is Bulldog-One, over." The colonel must have been in the helicopter as his voice was jarring during the call.

LG handed Sixpack the handset and he quickly responded, "This is Sierra-One-Six, go ahead, Bulldog-One."

"Be advised that we're up above the camp and have a decent view of most of it as the artillery and Air Force opened up much of the area. We can see a handful of destroyed bunkers and exposed tunneling through the area. The hootches pretty much burned themselves out but their structures remain. One thing for sure, it's much bigger than you suspected as it extends beyond the destroyed area. We'll have our hands full going through this mess. Sierra-Actual is coming out with the rest of Alpha and will assume control on the ground when they arrive."

This meant Captain Fowler would be taking the lead, which was good news.

"What's this 'we'll' shit?" Sixpack thought. "He can't get too dirty flying around up there."

"Roger, Bulldog. What do you want us to do until they get here?"

"Stay in place, One-Six. ETA for Alpha and Charlie is about an hour. A mechanized platoon from First of the Fifth should also arrive, but sooner than everyone else."

"Wilco, Sierra-One-Six, standing by."

Sixpack relayed the information from the colonel to the troops. With all the bodies coming, almost two full companies of men and four APCs would be together here on the ground, which pleased the men.

Thirty minutes later, they heard diesel engines and crashing sounds coming from the south as the metal beasts bulldozed their way along the stream. The noise reverberated through the canopy and increased in volume as they neared.

Sixpack gathered the platoon and moved out of their hide, closer to the raging stream.

After several minutes, the first APC came crashing through the foliage, rocking from side to side as it tracked over the debris it created. Six soldiers perched on top: one sat in a cupola manning a 50-caliber machine gun, the others sat precariously along the sides, holding onto rails running the length of the machine. The tracked vehicle moved another 50 feet before stopping abruptly and turning toward the stream. The remaining three tracks, each manned like the first, broke out of the foliage and grouped into a staggered formation facing the river.

The soldiers exchanged peace signs with one another in passing; black troops raised their fists in salute to the brothers in both platoons.

Sixpack and LG walked over to the first track.

A Second Lieutenant jumped off and greeted the two men. "Sierra-One-Six, I presume."

"Roger that."

"I'm Striker-Two-Actual." Both men shook hands. "Where's this basecamp we're supposed to check out?"

Sixpack pointed across the stream and toward the trail leading away. "About a hundred meters up that way."

"You expect trouble?"

"Not sure. It's a huge camp. We dropped Arty on them, Cobras worked over the area, and a flight of bombers dropped several 500 pounders on them."

Hearing the circling helicopter, the lieutenant looked up. "One of yours?"

"Yep. Our battalion CO is flying in the chopper and said the camp was pretty much destroyed. We haven't received any return fire or seen movement since our initial encounter."

"Seems odd if it's as big as you say."

"Yeah, surprised us, too. Hopefully, the bad guys aren't dug in and waiting for us as we walk in. This will be our first time inside."

"You get a lot of casualties?"

"Not a one!"

"Now that is odd!" The lieutenant looked toward the idling beasts. "Okay, I'm going to give my guys a break. Let me know when the captain gets here."

"Will do."

The two leaders turned and headed toward their respective platoons.

The officer gave the order to kill the engines and dismount. The soldiers jumped off, stretched, and walked toward the stream. Once there, most of them bent over and splashed the cool water over their heads and faces to remove the diesel soot. The gunners stayed in their cupolas and continued to scan the area on the other side of the stream.

For some of the Alpha soldiers, this was the first time they saw mechanized troop carriers. Some stood in awe of the tracks.

"Never worked with armor before."

"Those guys got it made."

Sixpack laughed. "Did you see everybody riding on top when they arrived?"

The short-timers smirked while the newbies appeared confused.

"They don't have to hump and carry supplies on their backs. That's already a cushy job."

"Those are iron coffins," Sixpack said matter-of-factly. "Every enemy soldier within a mile can hear them coming. All they have to do is mine the approach and wait for your APC to blow its track. Then he'll finish you off with either a B-40 rocket or RPG. I've seen what they can do to those armored tracks. Everything inside is cut to ribbons. It might look appealing, but you can have them."

"I thought they were bulletproof."

"They are against small arms, but they're just another thin-walled tin can when the big stuff comes out."

"Well then, maybe they don't have it so good."

Just then LG alerted Sixpack of a call. "Sierra-One-Six this is Sierra-Actual, over."

"This is One-Six, go ahead."

"We're in two columns following the eastbound trail and should arrive at your location within ten minutes."

"Good copy. Standing by."

"Sierra-One-Six, this is Kilo-One-Actual on your push." Charlie Company had dialed onto Alpha's frequency and were checking in.

"Go ahead Kilo-One-Actual."

"Roger, we're also about ten minutes away from your position and will be coming in from your north."

"Good copy, Kilo-One-Actual."

"Friendlies coming up this trail and along the river!" Sixpack alerted the soldiers and used hand signals showing the direction they would be coming from. "Pass the word."

Close to 125 soldiers converged on the intersection of the eastbound trail and the blue line to join the two platoons already there. Alpha's point men were the first to break through the tangle of vegetation on both sides of the trail; 75 additional soldiers followed closely as they exited onto the hard-packed trail. The First Platoon soldiers quickly greeted their brothers-in-arms. They managed to spread out along the trail and take a break after the difficult hump. Captain Fowler stepped out from the group and moved toward the stream where Sixpack waited.

"You guys got any food for us?" The request from the First Platoon went up and down the line of soldiers.

"Hell yeah!" The newly arrived soldiers were told to pack extra meals at the firebase before they left. All opened their rucksacks and pulled out boxed C-Ration meals, passed them forward and placed them in a pile in the center of the trail.

"Sixpack, have your men gather supplies and take a break while the lieutenants and I make plans."

"Will do, Captain."

Just then, the soldiers from Charlie Company arrived, the two platoons walking in a single file on the hard packed trail along the stream. They too, stopped and sat in place once close enough to the others.

The First Platoon troops grabbed a meal box from the pile, and returned to their guard positions. None were concerned about their meal choice, only glad to have some sustenance after going so long without. All meals would be eaten cold, but none of the soldiers cared. Another Kit Carson Scout in the company carried Nung's rucksack from Lynch and presented it to him. He was overjoyed and grinned like it was Christmas morning. His rucksack was full of delicious Vietnamese choices. He offered some to his fellow soldiers, but nobody took him up on his generous offer.

"Can anybody make some hot water for coffee and cocoa?" an appeal sounded from the jungle.

"We can help there." One of the soldiers from the APC Platoon pulled out a 5-gallon metal container from inside his track, placed it on three large stones, broke off a portion of C4 from a bar, lit it and tossed it under the container. The fire burned hot and fast and within a minute boiling water erupted from the nozzle. He used a pair of asbestos gloves to handle the red-hot container. Sixpack and his platoon made their way to the track carrying empty canteen cups. Each C-ration box had coffee and cocoa packets within; the men celebrated their good fortune.

After the soldiers had their fill, Capt. Fowler and the remaining three First Lieutenants of Alpha Company, a lone brown bar from Charlie, and the armor First Lieutenant convened just inside of the jungle with Sixpack and listened to him explain the events of the day. The captain discussed the mission with the colonel and then passed on the plans and order of march to the other officers.

The colonel still circled overhead anxiously awaiting the events to unfold.

Captain Fowler's plan was for the armored unit to remain on this side of the stream along with the two platoons of Charlie Company to provide rear security and be in reserve. Alpha Company would get online and then cross the stream while the APCs provided covering fire overhead. They would stop firing once Alpha reached the top of the rise, prepared to enter the camp proper and sweep across to the other side.

On a signal, the APCs opened fire with their 50s and 60s, traversing the area to their front. During the mad minute, the first of Alpha Company's soldiers had crossed the stream and reached the small draw near the top. They waited in a defensive posture until the tracks ceased fire.

Camouflaged netting hung from the tree branches and created a barrier for the soldiers, surprising them.

"What the fuck is this shit?"

"Use your knives and cut through," the suggestion passed down the line.

The troops unsheathed Bowie Knives and K-Bars, which they all carried, and cut their way through the netting.

"If there's anybody in there, they sure as shit know we're coming with all the racket we're making."

"This is some heavy-duty shit. Too bad those tracks didn't have a fire breathing dragon with them."

"Too late now."

Once the first wave of soldiers was through the netting, they found the ground bare of vegetation and hard packed.

"This place has been here forever."

"Keep the chatter down!" a squad leader chastised.

Several huts on the south side of the camp stood in ruins and still smoldering. The western boundary had several well concealed bunkers along its length; all but a couple were destroyed. Several fighting trenches zigzagged from bunker to bunker to beef up the camp's defense if attacked.

The remains of hammocks full of holes and in tattered pieces hung from nearby trees. Cooking fires smoldered; embers still glowing. Cooking utensils, pots and loose rice littered the ground everywhere.

An area in the center appeared to be a training area with remains of a small stage and several rows of ammo boxes for attending troops. The remnants of a green chalkboard and pieces of chalk lay among the ruins.

Not only were there bunkers on the perimeter of the camp, but several others were located strategically within the camp proper and encircled a much larger bunker in the center of the compound; a second defensive ring surrounding the headquarters bunker.

The southern portion of the camp was now exposed from overhead as the trees initially providing camouflage lay in pieces throughout the area. Eight large craters marked where the bombs landed when the jets dropped their ordinance. Smaller craters interspersed among them from the 105mm cannons fired from the firebase.

"Will you look at that," BJ announced, pointing upward. "They tied the trees together and used netting so nobody could see them from overhead."

Polack was in awe. "Damn! I wonder how they did that."

"They're probably in cahoots with the rock apes," Wild Bill proffered.

Those nearby chuckled while continuing their sweep of the camp. Even Polack smiled broadly.

Netting hung from overhead and fell to the ground like a waterfall. The damage, however, only impacted half of the camp as it extended north beyond where Sgt. Rock's squad was fired upon. There, the bunkers and ground were still intact, requiring a more personal inspection.

From up above, the colonel kept asking if any confirmed bodies had been found yet.

Those on the ground ignored him and troops continued sweeping through the area.

The northern portion of the camp was a mirrored version of the destroyed southern side. Two of the larger huts still intact were identified as hospitals. Medical equipment and medicine were stored in cabinets. Hammocks hung in rows only a couple feet above the ground, and beds made from bamboo and vines lined the walls. The second hut contained two operating rooms and a single treatment room. Here, blood had pooled on the ground and dried to a rust-colored blanket atop the blackened earth. Blood-soaked U.S. Army stretchers were also found in both huts.

Two ammo bunkers on the northeast side of the compound were organized and filled with crates of 7.62mm ammunition, AK-47 magazines, mortar and RPG rounds, belts of ammo and circular magazines for machine guns, wood handled grenades, anti-personnel mines, and cases of weapons.

Nung exited excitedly from a third larger bunker nearby carrying a stalk of bananas. "Sargin Homes, come see, beaucoup chop-chop."

As the squad approached, Nung broke off a banana and tossed one to each of the men as they approached. Nung led them inside and pointed out the bounty in the mostly underground warehouse.

"This place is huge!"

"Bigger than our tent back at the firebase."

Dozens of 50-pound bags of rice were stacked against one of the walls, tinned meats, vegetables, and fruit were stacked in rows on shelves. Fish lay in pans fermenting, bananas and bags of other fruit hung from the ceiling. No tunnel led out of this bunker, but a cot sat on the opposite wall, with a month-old Vietnamese magazine and musical instruments lying haphazardly upon it. Nung picked up one of several flutes carved from bamboo and played notes of a catchy tune.

"Not bad, Nung. Play some more."

"Maybe later in firebase." The Kit Carson Scout smiled broadly and placed it into his pants pocket. Next, he pointed to two brown hardwood pieces of wood measuring four inches by eight inches and a quarter inch thick with matching pencil-like sticks. He picked up the sticks and showed how to use them as drums to control the beat. Still smiling, he dropped the sticks and then picked up a long-necked banjo looking thing with raised frets and only two strings. Strumming it sounded like an off-key, untuned child's plastic guitar with nylon strings. Setting it against the wall, he walked over to what looked like a xylophone made with bamboo tubes. Nung demonstrated the instrument which sounded like a woodpecker knocking against different sized tree trunks. Bowing to the troops, Nung said, "Baby-san come sing and make numba one music for VC."

"You mean like bands?" BJ asked.

"Yah, bans. Go camp to camp."

On the way out, the men grabbed another banana from the stalks hanging from the roof of the bunker.

Sixpack gathered the squad outside the bunker, "I'm going to find the captain and let him know what we found here. Most likely he'll want us to count everything and pile it all outside. Hang loose here till I get back."

The men sat and leaned against the bunker, everyone lighting up cigarettes.

"You believe that shit?" Wild Bill said, "Musical instruments for a traveling band."

"Unreal," Scout added. "We don't get traveling bands at our firebases."

"Maybe Uncle Ho visits like Bob Hope does us," Frenchie commented.

This resulted in guffaws from the others.

Nung pointed to the entrance of the bunker, "Numba one chop-chop. We take for us."

Wild Bill responded, "That's all gook shit and probably older than our C-Rations. It's all yours, Nung."

When everyone agreed, Nung dashed back inside.

The tunnel rats explored underground and discovered a command center complete with a military radio, wall maps, transistor radios, and various documents. This turned out to be a treasure trove for the intelligence community and they would take every bit of evidence with them.

The camp was almost as large as a football field. Several trails led away into the jungle all around the compound so those escaping could have gone in any direction.

Sixpack returned from his visit with the captain and new orders for the platoon. "We're going to scope out the trails leading to the east from here. Charlie Company's Platoons will check out the north, and Third Platoon will check out the south. Everybody else will stay behind to provide security and do whatever the colonel needs done."

"No breaks for the wicked," Scout chimed in.

Sixpack ignored the comment. "There's a dog team, an intel group, and engineers coming in on the next bird to take care of things around here."

As the men were getting to their feet, Nung exited the bunker, and waddled toward them, his pockets bulging and filled with dozens of metal tins.

"Hold it right there, Nung. You're not taking all that shit with you on this patrol."

Nung looked perplexed and raised his arms in defeat. "Numba one chop-chop for GI, will last beaucoup time."

"I know, Nung, but you can't take it with you."

"Which way we go?"

Sixpack pointed to the east. "That way."

Nung surveyed the area and hobbled in the direction that Sixpack had pointed. Once outside the camp boundary, he emptied his pockets onto the ground and covered his stash with a couple banana leaves. Smiling at his success, he returned and told Sixpack, "Nung ready!"

The colonel was getting antsy flying overhead and wanted to be on the ground to witness the find. He ordered the mechanized platoon to cross the stream and come into the basecamp. They carried crates of C-4 explosive that could be used to knock down trees and create a landing zone within the camp itself; he wanted one large enough to accommodate two helicopters. Most of the terrain was barren and only a select number of trees had to be blown to clear the way. Some of the thinner trunk trees were knocked over by the metal beasts as they moved to the other side of the basecamp. Blocks of C4, det cord, blasting caps and axes were distributed to the remaining Alpha Company soldiers who went about clearing out the brush.

The First Platoon broke into squad sized units and would each follow one of the four larger trails leading away from the camp. The ground was pocked with boot prints and scuff marks, evidence that a large group moved quickly through the area. The prints were shallow indicating that the soldiers were moving lightly and not carrying supplies with them.

Within 40 minutes, the men creating the landing zone completed their task and assumed positions around the perimeter. Soon after, the Colonel was on the ground, marveling at his good fortune.

Each of the four squads of the First Platoon continued to follow the boot prints along the four-foot wide trails. The well-used paths like many others mimicked walking through a tunnel of vegetation with a seven-foot high ceiling. Wild scrub brush lined both sides and held back the thick jungle growth. Any attempt to leave the trail and duck into the side jungle cover would be obvious. The parade of boot prints and scuffling continued, on all four trails, far beyond their one-click limit without exposing the enemy. Sixpack called off the hunt and the men turned back.

A platoon of Charlie Company used the same strategy on their patrol and did come across several blood trails along two of the largest trails. Of course, these trails were also the closest to the hospital huts so most likely these were used to evacuate the patients and walking wounded. The blood trails soon dried up and they, too, found no new evidence of the evading enemy. They called it quits after a little more than a click and returned to the basecamp.

Third Platoon of Alpha Company spread out and followed trails leading out from the south side of the camp. Unlike the others, they came across seven dead enemy soldiers within the first 100 meters. All carried either an AK-47 or SKS bolt action rifle. Some wore rucksacks and ammo vests, pith helmets spilled onto the ground and laid where they fell. Two shirtless bodies wore nothing but a pair of undershorts. The bodies were not grouped together and fell out as singles along a portion of the trail. The nearest bodies to the camp were killed by artillery, pieces of shrapnel, some as large as a fist; others, the size of peas, peppered their backs. Those farther away appeared to be killed by bullets fired from the gunships as the bodies were hit multiple times. One body stood vertical on the side of the trail as if he stopped by a small tree to catch his breath, then died standing up. His right arm caught in the crook of a limb and the soldier looked to be leaning face first into the tree trunk.

One grunt remarked, "Check him out, looks like he's counting off in a game of hide and seek."

Some of the soldiers chuckled while others just shook their heads and rolled their eyes.

The platoon continued in its quest to locate the enemy with the intent to police up any supplies on their way back to the camp.

After one click, they too, called it quits. During their trek, they crossed over the waist-deep stream four times as it snaked east and south along the way. They would have to repeat the process on the way back.

Almost three hours passed since the patrols left the camp. Returning would be much quicker. During their return trips, loud explosions boomed and continued to their front, the engineers busy blowing up bunkers and tunnels.

First Platoon was the first of the patrols to return. The colonel's C&C Huey and a second helicopter were both parked in the newly created landing zone. The full-bird and several other officers were examining items brought up from the underground command center. Overhead, two Cobra helicopters flew lazy circles, on guard and waiting patiently in the event they were requested to unleash their fury.

The two ammunition and food storage bunkers were in ruins, their bounty removed and evacuated earlier to Cu Chi by helicopter.

Same with the medical huts which now smoldered after burning to the ground.

When the rest of Alpha Company exited the jungle from the south, two of the men sported wide grins and proudly waved SKS rifles in the air. Since these were single bolt action weapons, the captured rifles were authorized as war souvenirs and could be taken home by soldiers. Unfortunately for these two, once the souvenirs left for the rear, they would never be seen again.

The four captured rucksacks, ammo vests, and AK-47 rifles were dropped in a pile by the helicopter. Several of the enemy soldiers also wore pith helmets designated as war souvenirs. Four soldiers strapped them to the back of their rucksacks.

Nung wasted no time and headed toward the discarded khaki-colored rucksacks. Picking one, he dumped everything out and carried it to where he hid his earlier stash. After a few moments, Nung exited the jungle wearing both a bulging rucksack and a shit-eating grin.

Word spread among the troops that the documents uncovered from the tunnel complex confirmed that the camp was a regional headquarters for the Ninth Division, 272nd VC Regiment. In addition to the maps which included the location of FSB's Lynch, Frenzel Jones, Kien, and a few nearby Australian camps, there were also detailed sketches of those firebases. Other documents listed the names of double agents within Saigon and Vung Tau. The members of the intel group frothed at the mouth for what they considered a motherlode of information.

This was indeed a staging station where incoming soldiers from the Ho Chi Minh Trail rested, ate decent food, trained, and treated their maladies of the jungle after their months-long march from North Vietnam. Afterwards, their trek to Saigon and provinces to the east and south would continue.

"Why do you suppose they ran off instead of standing firm and fighting us?"

"BJ, gooks always choose the time and place to fight and will do so if they have the advantage." Wild Bill scratched his face where a growth of beard covered his chin and cheeks. "I guess in this case they didn't think they could win."

"Maybe they were all new Cherries and haven't been in a firefight yet."

"Anything's possible, Scout. I'm only glad they did."

"Hell, any survivors had the entire night to get away."

"Ain't that the truth!"

"It's just strange that they left all this shit behind."

Calls of 'Fire in the hole' continued through the camp, followed by explosions from the north side of the camp where engineers continued blowing up bunkers and connecting trenches.

Members of Charlie Company carried supplies and boxes of documents to stack inside the second helicopter, including the stash that Alpha Company brought back with them. Every item of interest had already been brought topside from the command bunker below ground and engineers were in the process of setting charges to blow the tunnel complex sky-high. Meanwhile, a dozen or so soldiers had collected and carried the 16 dead enemy bodies uncovered by the dog team from around the camp. They found most in the already destroyed bunkers on the south side of the complex, unceremoniously dropped into one of the trenches and covered with dirt. Captain Fowler decided to leave the seven bodies where they fell on the trail outside of the camp.

The colonel looked disappointed that they had only uncovered 23 enemy bodies from a camp of this size. His face was twisted in a snarl as he boarded the chopper. His staff, however, was quite pleased with their finds and still chattered away excitedly. After a minute, the C&C chopper rose straight up and the second helicopter followed as they headed southeast and flew back to Cu Chi.

At 1600 hours Captain Fowler dismissed the mechanized platoon. They cranked up their engines, crossed back over the stream, and headed out the way they came.

Soldiers riding on top moved their upper bodies around to counter the move of the metal beast as it tipped side to side.

The two platoons of Charlie Company were also sent back to the firebase, and gambling fate, they chose to follow the western trail: the same trail one of their platoons had been ambushed on a couple days earlier. This way, they could get back more quickly than going back the way they came.

Captain Fowler gathered the four platoon leaders and laid out his plan.

"Spread your men out. We're going to provide security until the engineers pull out. They already demolished everything above ground and are preparing to blow the tunnel complex with a timed fuse. I'll get word to you when it's time to go."

The men dispersed and headed toward their troops who then fanned out around the perimeter of the destroyed basecamp.

Within 30 minutes, a lone helicopter landed on the makeshift landing zone. The four engineers gathered their equipment and scampered aboard. "You got thirty minutes," the lead engineer told Captain Fowler. "Get your men out of here." With that, the bird rose into the canopy and circled high above the camp remaining on station until after the explosion.

The 103 soldiers of Alpha Company gathered quickly and followed along the same trail Charlie Company had used. After 200 meters, the captain directed the column to turn off the trail and form a perimeter in the jungle on the south side of the trail.

The captain, his lieutenants, and Sixpack gathered in the center.

"We're going to stay here tonight."

"What about supplies for the First Platoon?" Sixpack asked. Other than their weapons and ammo, they had nothing else.

"We've got enough to share. Shouldn't be a problem," the three lieutenants said in unison.

"Good," the captain continued. "Tomorrow early, we'll send in some folks to check out the blown tunnel complex, leave some mechanical ambushes, and then return to the firebase."

The engineering chopper was still flying circles overhead when an RTO called out, "Fire in the hole in one minute."

Everyone within the perimeter hugged the ground making certain they had enough cover, counting down from sixty in their heads.

Even at 300 meters, the eruption was so savage, the ground shook like an earthquake and debris rained down upon the men. Clumps of dirt landed with a 'plop' surprising some of the soldiers who closed their eyes during the black and red dirt snowfall. A smell of sulfur permeated the air as the spent explosive blossomed into a giant fireball, rolling through the overhead foliage and high into the empty sky. Seconds later, a dust cloud formed and drifted outward from the camp, but a breeze from the west kept it from encapsulating the Alpha troops.

"Looks good from up here," the call came across the radio. "We're going to head out. Be safe down there." The sound of the rotors diminished as the chopper turned south east and headed back to Cu Chi.

Once the threat passed, Captain Fowler continued his discussion.

"Sixpack, have the First Platoon buddy up with somebody on the perimeter, and share their food, water, and ponchos during the night."

"Roger that."

"It'll be dark in an hour so have your men put out Claymores and trip flares around the perimeter. Sixpack, have your men set a couple of mechanical ambushes out on the trail either side of our position."

"See my guys," the Third Platoon Lieutenant volunteered, looking directly at Sixpack. "They've got the supplies you'll need."

Sixpack acknowledged with a head nod.

"Tomorrow, First Platoon will head into the basecamp and conduct a quick recon to make sure everything was thoroughly destroyed. Once that's done, we'll head back to Lynch."

With that said, the leaders returned to their men and set the plans in motion.

The members of the First Platoon had no problem finding a buddy. They all knew one another but seldom had an opportunity to be together in the bush. It was supposed to be a quiet night.

Polack had another nightmare that night, moaning and continuously turning over.

He and LG were attacked by rock apes, hairy and Sasquatch-looking. They were seven feet tall, stout, and very muscular. Their hair ranged from red, orange, brown, and black in color, covering everywhere except for their knees, the soles of their feet, hands, and face. These beasts threw large rocks at the two of them and more were hitting their target consistently. Rocks came in like fastballs at a ballpark. The darkness of night hid everything and being hit felt like a sucker punch. The apes screeched loudly during the attack and there was no escaping their onslaught, no matter how hard the men tried.

His bunk buddy, James, an African American from Mobile, Alabama was alarmed by Polack's sudden outburst. When he placed his hand over his mouth and tried to shake him awake, his hands came back wet from Polack's heavy sweating.

"Come on, brother. Wake up, you're dreaming."

Others nearby stirred and woke because of the disturbance.

"Polack! Polack!" James slapped him across the face, the shock brought him out of his stupor.

Polack's eyes opened and darted from side to side. He shook his head to clear the cobwebs and finally sat up.

"What happened?" Polack asked, still disoriented, and using his towel to wipe his face.

"You had a bad dream, bro."

Thinking for a moment. "Yeah, I remember now. Those rock apes were attacking me and LG, and almost killed us."

"No rock apes around here, brother." James handed his canteen over to him, "Here, drink some water, you'll feel better."

"Thanks, bro." He handed the canteen back and sat there for a few moments before lying back on the hard ground. He fell back asleep quickly.

Chapter Seven

In the morning, First Platoon left the night defensive position right after breakfast and headed to the former enemy complex with enough supplies to build four mechanical ambushes. Captain Fowler wanted to set booby traps within the camp to dissuade the enemy from returning. The rest of the company stayed put until their return.

Sixpack picked the Third and Fourth Squads to set the mechanical booby traps in the former camp, while he and the remaining two squads would wait at the trail junction by the stream.

Groans and comments arose from the 13 soldiers when they entered the stream and crossed using the underwater bridge, as cold water leaked into their boots.

"Our feet just dried from yesterday. Now we gotta hump it back to Lynch with wet feet."

"Thanks, Sixpack!"

"Lifer cocksuckers always got to fuck with us."

"Fuck it! Don't mean nuthin'"

"See ya in a skosh," someone called from one of the squads remaining behind.

When the patrol disappeared over the incline and into the camp proper, Sixpack had the rest of his men set a small perimeter covering the trails. They settled onto the ground and lit cigarettes, knowing that the patrol would be gone for at least 30 minutes.

Sixpack paced nervously back and forth along the river, checking his watch every few moments. Something in his gut just felt off. He made a mental note to blow the underwater bridge after the two squads returned.

Back at the NDP, many of the men took this potential hour-long pause as an opportunity to write letters, read books, or just crash; the first such chance in a week.

Captain Fowler informed Bulldog-One that the morning detail was underway, and that troops were expected back within the hour. He, too, pulled out a piece of paper and began a letter to his wife.

Suddenly, the sound of gunfire from the direction of the base camp shattered the serenity. Without hesitation, the rest of Alpha Company troops snatched up web gear, ammunition, and weapons, then hustled out to the trail in support of their fellow soldiers fighting in the base camp.

Sixpack and his 14 soldiers also reacted quickly, crossing the stream and moving up to the camp perimeter, spreading out in the jungle foliage along the western side.

They first noticed that both squads had jumped into the ruins of two different bunkers and were pinned down by the enemy. Adding support from this vantage point would be too much of a risk as the trapped men sat directly in their line of fire.

Enemy soldiers fired from three repaired bunkers on the northern side of the complex. The trapped soldiers neither saw nor heard reinforcements but hoped they were nearby. They shouted and screamed loudly from their location to let the rest of the company know their location.

Sixpack's group was still about 50 feet away and luckily remained unnoticed by the enemy soldiers who focused on the two ruined bunkers with the Americans inside. The staff sergeant had his men skirt north along the outside of the perimeter, purposely holding their fire until they had unobstructed lines of fire. Just then, the deep sound of an enemy machine gun joined the firefight.

Sixpack apprised the captain of the situation and drew a mental picture for him over the radio.

When he arrived at the trail intersection with the rest of the company, the captain directed two platoons to work their way around the perimeter until reaching the eastern side, then move north to flank the enemy. The remaining platoon linked up with Sixpack along the western perimeter in hopes of catching the enemy in a crossfire.

Of course, it was difficult for 60 grunts to remain stealthy while encircling the camp. With the noise of them rustling through the foliage and then periodically exposing themselves, the enemy caught sight of their movement and opened fire on them.

Gunships arrived in response to Sixpack's request for support but they were unable to help because of their close proximity of the enemy. The only solution was to rescue the pinned down squads and then move away to a safe distance so the gunships could use their miniguns and rockets.

The troops along the western perimeter continued to hold their fire as they edged into position. Still unnoticed, they continued to spread out along and below the incline until the men had unobstructed views of the enemy.

The soldiers along the south and portions of the east perimeter found themselves in a precarious situation as they tried to move through a quagmire of felled trees, branches, and other debris from past shelling and air attacks. They were trapped, having been in constant contact with the enemy since their discovery. Any soldiers rising to move over the large logs and debris provided the enemy with an easy target. On the other hand, they had excellent cover providing they remained in place.

Sixpack ordered the machine gun teams to find defendable positions in the foliage along the western front. Once everyone was ready and a signal given, every Alpha Company troop around the perimeter opened fire on the three bunkers.

The added weapons completely surprised the enemy soldiers, as well as those in the besieged bunkers. The enemy recovered quickly and adjusted their fields of fire, keeping the Americans pinned down.

Those in the besieged bunkers hollered their support.

A short pause in the firing allowed Sixpack to call out his plan to the men in the closest bunker then waited while they relayed it to the other squad 30 feet farther and more toward the center of the compound. Those in the nearest bunker also communicated that two of their men were hurt. The injuries were not serious and the soldiers could move with some assistance.

The platoon joining Sixpack's two squads brought two LAWs (disposable anti-tank missiles) which they would fire at the enemy bunkers. The subsequent explosion would be the signal for everyone around the perimeter to open fire on full-automatic hoping that it was enough to keep the enemy heads down, allowing the trapped soldiers to escape toward the perimeter.

The LAWs blew large holes into two of the shelters but failed to fully silence the guns inside. Nearby grunts aimed and fired through the new holes and exposed firing slots, hoping for a lucky shot or ricochet to silence them.

Alpha troops fired steadily for about 30 seconds, yet no movement occurred from the trapped men in the nearest bunker. For some reason, they had ignored the signal to vacate the bunkers.

Those soldiers in the second bunker exited as instructed and low crawled toward the west perimeter, moving diagonally to keep the vacated bunker between themselves and the enemy. Shouts from the perimeter encouraged the men onward.

"C'MON, HURRY, YOU GOT THIS!"

Those in the nearest bunker remained inside.

"Don't those fuckers know they're supposed to be coming out during this cover fire? What the fuck's their problem?" Wild Bill called loudly to Polack, who had already fired 200 rounds on the machine gun during the last minute.

"Dammit guys, we can't keep this up forever!" Wild Bill called out. "Un-ass that bunker, come on!"

The last soldier from the second bunker reached the perimeter and crawled over Scout's prone body, then rolled down the incline to safety.

The level of fire dropped significantly to conserve ammunition.

Suddenly, Wild Bill rose from behind his tree and bolted across the barren terrain. Puffs of dirt erupted on the ground all around him as he zigzagged toward the bunker and dove headfirst through the opening. Those nearby could hear Wild Bill chastising the troops inside.

Firing, once again, intensified after the troops witnessed the bravery displayed by one of their own. The bunker had no roof but still provided adequate cover provided no one stood up. All at once, several hand grenades and two smoke grenades arced out of the wreckage toward the enemy. They landed way short of their intended target and exploded harmlessly. The smoke grenades, however, would blind the enemy for a short period of time. Seconds later, one by one, six men emerged from the bunker, stooped over, running wildly toward the safety of the western perimeter. Wild Bill was the last to step out with a man laying across his shoulders in a fireman's carry; he fired at the enemy one-handed, while racing across the 30 feet of open ground. The men watching this rescue gawked at his bravery and focused on keeping the enemy's head down until they reached safety. Once clear, Sixpack tossed a red smoke grenade as far as he could and had everyone withdraw to the trail intersection.

The captain gave the gunships an all clear and two Cobra helicopters started their runs on the bunker complex using the red smoke as a beacon. As the rockets and miniguns fired, the company of soldiers retreated to their NDP, where the CP requested both a Medivac for the two wounded soldiers and a resupply of ammo.

When the gunships exhausted their ordinance and fuel, artillery took over in the interim, pounding at the complex until the gunships returned with a fresh load of ordinance.

While they waited for the Medivac, the two rescued squad leaders sat with Sixpack and the captain to explain how they got into the predicament at the enemy basecamp.

Calvin began, "When we walked into the ruins, we split into two teams. Mine moved toward the north while Willy's squad went more toward the center. We were almost in place to set our mechanicals when I spotted repairs on a couple bunkers ahead and stopped the patrol."

Willy chimed in, "I noticed the bunkers at the same time and had everybody take a knee. That's when I spotted a small campfire with a pot of boiling water hung above the flame. I whispered to my guys that we weren't alone and needed to get the fuck out of Dodge. We started to di-di toward the perimeter when an enemy soldier popped up and spotted us. He yelled out a warning and fired a burst of AK at us. We were lucky to be so close to a bunker and all jumped in."

Calvin continued his story, "We weren't spotted at first when they opened fire on Willy and his crew, but they saw us the minute we got up and moved toward the outer perimeter. When they took us under fire, it sounded like dozens of AKs were shooting at us. We'd have never made it to the perimeter and, instead, jumped into a trashed bunker like Willy's team did and returned fire on them."

"How did your guys get hurt?"

"Spence caught it in the shoulder moving to the bunker, and Julius twisted his knee when he jumped inside."

"Willy, why didn't your team come out when they were supposed to?"

The soldier bowed his head and clenched his teeth. Glancing up, he could not even look the captain in the eye. "Our doorway faced the gooks and we didn't think any of us would make it. We were scared and nobody wanted to be the first one out." Willy's eyes glossed over and he buried his head in his green towel.

"That delay could have caused others to get hurt."

"I'm sorry, Sixpack." He looked directly into the sergeant's eyes, "Thank God for people like Wild Bill. We owe him big time!"

Calvin reached over and put his arm around Willy and pulled him tight. "That's okay, bro. It happens to all of us." Willy hugged him back.

"Okay, you guys can head back to your squads and catch your breath."

The two men stood up, hammered Sixpack's fist with their own and headed back to their teams.

"It's a miracle that's all the injuries we sustained." Captain Fowler finished his notes, closed his small notebook, and returned it to his chest pocket.

Both soldiers were evacuated by jungle penetrator and taken to the 93rd Evac Hospital in Long Binh.

The assault on the former base camp continued for what seemed like an hour, the gunships and artillery alternating fire. Finally, Captain Fowler called for a cease fire and ordered the men online at the stream to sweep the camp again.

Prior to entering the complex, one platoon fired its weapons into the general direction of the bunkers for 30 seconds. There was no return fire so the men moved cautiously toward their objective. The First Platoon, especially those from the two trapped squads, were hoping the enemy soldiers had vacated the complex as before; one narrow escape was enough for the day.

Once inside the perimeter, platoon leaders immediately dispatched half their men into the surrounding jungle to secure the perimeter while the remainder searched through the rubble.

The damage was much more intense this time as the fire concentrated on only a small portion of the camp. Once again, they encountered no resistance during the sweep, but the results were much different. They counted 16 bodies, most found inside and around the three bunkers; and four more located on a nearby trail outside of the perimeter, presumably killed while attempting to flee the devastation. The four soldiers killed outside of the perimeter wore NVA uniforms, while the remaining corpses sported typical VC black pajamas and Ho Chi Minh sandals; an AK-47 rifle lay within reach of each body. The troops also discovered two ruined RPD machine guns in two of the rebuilt bunkers.

Nearby, a large quantity of tools to help in rebuilding the camp: pickaxes, shovels, rakes, hoes, saws, and axes lay in pieces.

The only American casualties were the two men from Fourth Squad.

The grunts searched the dead bodies, collecting everything of importance, sending rucksacks, ammo vests, documents, weapons, and unbroken tools back to Cu Chi on a lone chopper. The colonel, ecstatic hearing the news of additional body counts, suggested that the company hang around for another day and ambush the surrounding trails. After some heated discussion with the captain, the colonel changed his mind and approved their return to Lynch.

The company left four mechanical ambushes on trails leading into the devastated camp and then walked out of the former basecamp for what they hoped was the last time. Sixpack also placed some C-4 on the underwater bridge in the stream. When it blew, the concussion threw water and bamboo up over the dry jungle for 100 feet; leaves fell from the canopy like a snowfall. Dead fish floated to the top of the water by the dozens before being immediately swept away by the current. The explosion also caused a pause in the chatter of the jungle inhabitants lasting several minutes. Then slowly, the shrieks, whistles, moans, grunts, and other sounds returned, soon rendering a symphony of sounds signaling to everyone that the danger passed. The overpowering smell of cordite and smoke would soon dissipate, the area reverting to the everyday smell of rotting vegetation.

Wild Bill was later awarded the Bronze Star with a "V" device for Valor in his actions during the ambush at the enemy base camp. His snap decision to rescue the trapped soldiers from that bunker had potentially saved many lives. He later said that he did it so they could all get the hell out of there. He insisted that he did not intend for his actions to be heroic; he was merely "impatient" and wanted to get back to Lynch.

Chapter Eight

One hundred one soldiers straddled the main east-west trail, chopping their way through the bush, keeping about 10 feet from the trail. Soldiers were also dispatched to their flanks. As First Platoon soldiers had no rucksacks, the hump was much easier for them. Knowing this, the captain delegated them to take point and cover the flanks. One squad led each column, and another flanked the company on each side. They snaked through the hanging vines and twisted underbrush, not using machetes for the most part, maintaining sight and keeping pace with the columns some 30 feet away. Every member in the company had wet feet from crossing the stream. Nobody carried spare socks, so some soldiers removed them and walked without. Feet squished inside boots with each step, however, no one complained as the problem would go away once they reached the firebase.

The men knew this was not a walk in the park and used extreme caution in their movements. This area, all within five clicks of the new firebase, would continue to be a thorn in their sides as enemy troops continued to travel through the area from Cambodia and the Ho Chi Minh Trail.

The men gently caressed welts, rashes, bruises, and mosquito bites while keeping their eyes on the surrounding jungle for the enemy.

When they reached the location where Charlie Company was ambushed, the troops took their first break. The evidence surrounded the men: blood trails, spent bullet casings, empty magazines, and grenade craters. No one dared to pick anything up in fear that it was booby trapped. Soon, all the evidence would be reclaimed by Mother Earth and covered by vegetation. The location itself was only important to those who almost died there.

The second break was called at the location of Rock's successful ambush. Here, it was much of the same except for the hollowed depressions where the Claymore Mines exploded, vegetation blown apart 20 feet around the dark black holes, spent brass casings littering the trail and immediate area. Rock and his squad gathered and reminisced about that night. Some examined the signs of the firefight, while those who did not closed their eyes during the short break.

Thirty minutes later, the columns broke out of the jungle and entered the Rome-plowed area surrounding the firebase. It was dry and much easier to move across the uneven ground. In sight of the firebase, silent shouts of relief echoed across the terrain from the soldiers. The firebase gave grunts a sense of security even if they were surrounded by a regiment of enemy soldiers.

The Alpha Company soldiers sweated profusely, their fatigue jackets and t-shirts darkened by moisture surrounding white splotches, of stiff, salty, stains of formerly dried sweat. Some soldiers draped towels over their heads resembling nuns for shade in their attempt to cool down in the hot afternoon sunshine. The men were ragged and worn out. Boots dragged across the ground, and soldiers too tired to walk normally, created a waist-high cloud of red dust that enveloped them as they moved across the plowed earth, reminiscent of Pigpen walking in the Charlie Brown cartoons.

"What's that smell?" The question was asked up and down the line as the soldiers neared the gate.

Thick black smoke rose into the air around the mess tent in the center of the compound, smelling of burnt grease and cooked meat.

Many of the soldiers raised their noses and sniffed the air as they moved through the gate and toward their platoon tents. "Smells like barbecue."

"I'm too tired to eat."

When the troops entered through the firebase gate, those inside manning the perimeter bunkers or loitering nearby welcomed them back as conquering heroes. Cheers arose and thankful words of encouragement showered the men.

The file of grunts could not help but smile and wave back wearily to their benevolent brothers in thanks.

The Fourth Platoon soldiers walked straight to an area used for cleaning weapons. Several tables held elongated half-barrels, improvised sinks which contained cleaning fluid several inches deep so the soldiers could soak and clean parts from their weapons. Red and blue hand towels were stacked in piles on the surrounding tables along with brushes, bore cleaners, and bottles of lubricating oil. Rucksacks were dropped and left where they fell around the tent; chatter resonated among the troops as they focused on cleaning their weapons.

First Platoon walked directly to their tent and entered their home away from home. Polack stood his M-60 nose down on the unfolded bipod legs next to the sandbagged wall and dropped onto his cot. "God, this feels good!"

There were no supplies to unload, as their rucksacks remained at the head of their cots leaning against the sandbagged walls where they were left three days ago. The tent canvas sidewalls were rolled up which allowed for a slight breeze to blow through the opened tent.

"Fuck it. Wake me tomorrow," Scout mumbled. His face buried in a poncho liner as he laid on his belly with arms hanging over the sides, fists only inches from the bare ground.

"Check out BJ, he's already snoring." Frenchie pointed to the sleeping soldier next to him and laughed deeply.

"Get it while you can. The lifers will probably stick us with bunker guard tonight." Wild Bill cajoled from his cot.

"Better not."

Of the 25 soldiers in the tent, all but a few were laying on their cots, exhausted after this last mission.

Still three hours before nightfall and the smell from the mess hall became more inviting as the minutes ticked on.

Sgt. Holmes suddenly entered the tent, weapon in hand and still dressed from the patrol. "Listen up, guys!" He walked along the aisle and kicked at a few pairs of boots hanging over the end of cots. The center aisle was now dry and red powder rose with each footstep. "I know we're all tired and want to crash, but there's stuff that needs to be done before we can do that."

"Come on Sixpack, let us sleep!"

"Yeah, cut us some slack!"

"You'll get a break afterwards. First thing on the agenda is to clean weapons and refill magazines with ammo. Once that's done, the mess tent is barbecuing hamburgers and hot dogs for us. The captain has also arranged for ice cream and two cold beers per person."

"Now you're talking." A couple guys sat up on their cots to hear what else Sixpack had to offer.

The sergeant continued, "You might also be interested in knowing that we now have two three-hole shitters on the bunker line and a two-spicket shower near the artillery pits. Clean towels and uniforms are also available. If you intend to take a shower, take a buddy with you."

"To do what, Sixpack? Wash my dick?"

The comment brought laughter from the weary soldiers.

"Only if that's your bag," Sixpack countered.

This brought additional guffaws from the men.

"The new shower uses overhead bags. There's also a water buffalo on wheels parked next to it. When you're ready to rinse, your buddy will dump a pail of water from the buffalo into the bag. Then when you're finished, return the favor so your buddy can shower."

"Sounds cool!"

"We also have the night off. No details or bunker guard. You guys are on your own until tomorrow when we get new orders."

This brought a smile to all the men and some cheers.

"Questions?"

There were none.

Sixpack turned and walked out of the tent, heading for the weapon cleaning tent. The First Platoon soldiers stirred and rose from their cots, gathering their weapons and following behind their Staff Sergeant.

"Polack, better wake BJ and explain what's happening."

"Already on it." Polack kicked BJ on the sole of his boots. The man stirred and turned onto his side. He then commenced to shake the cot until BJ's eyes opened and he responded. "What the fuck, Polack?"

He explained the situation, picked up the machine gun and then followed the others.

Replenishing ammo would be a breeze for Polack as he only had to carry a few cans of linked belts back to the tent. The others had to get bandoliers and strip bullets from the clips into magazines which took time.

A crowd was already gathered around the shower. Some waited for their turn under the cold, refreshing spray, while others stood only to watch and pass the time of day, like old men in a barbershop. No curtains or walls enclosed the structure so modesty was not an option.

The shitters were also devoid of walls or curtains to provide privacy. Three 55 gallon drums, cut in half, sat under a twenty-inch deep by ten-foot long wooden plank. Three oblong holes were spaced evenly across the face of the plank, sanded and smooth, one size fit all.

During the initial stages of building the firebase, these outhouses caused many problems. The main concern was the location, which sat on the edge of the perimeter next to the barbed wire. When using the facilities, you faced the inside of the perimeter leaving your back exposed to the jungle outside of the camp. This made it difficult to concentrate on the duties at hand, as the men continuously turned to keep an eye on the tree line.

Embarrassment was the other concern when trying to take care of business in plain view of everyone in the firebase. Many of the young men developed painful hemorrhoids from not letting nature take its course. They would purposely try to hold their bowel movements until nightfall, when the cover of darkness allowed them to relax in a more private manner.

Showers, clean clothes, a decent meal, dessert, and cold beer seemed to rejuvenate the soldiers and relieve pent-up stress. No details, bunker guard, and radio watch meant that this would be a rare opportunity to get eight or more hours of uninterrupted sleep for the First Platoon. Something they craved.

But, instead of crashing, the soldiers partied, wrote letters, read books, and played card games through much of the night. For them, it was a happy time, and a time to celebrate. They crushed the enemy and not one of them had to die.

In the near distance, troops could hear a lone flute playing. The tune, serene and calming, lulled some to sleep like a lullaby does a baby; their reward for surviving another mission in paradise.

Epilogue

The Iron Triangle was a painful thorn in the sides of the Americans, Aussies, and South Vietnamese Army during the entire war. The local VC regiments were basically wiped out during the 1968 Tet Offensive, but skilled NVA troops came down the trail and filled their depleted ranks.

Six months after this story took place, the 25th Infantry Division left Vietnam and returned to Hawaii. Their firebases were either destroyed beforehand or turned over to the South Vietnamese.

Throughout the war, South Vietnam and its allies failed to destroy the Viet Cong support system that had been built for decades in the Triangle.

In 1974, a year after the American military had left the war, the People's Army of Vietnam (NVA) invaded the south through the Iron Triangle. Pitched battles took place for over six months before the invaders were pushed back into Cambodia.

A year later, the NVA used the Iron Triangle again to orchestrate a final, decisive attack on Saigon that finally ended the war.

I hope you enjoyed my story, and I would appreciate if you could take few moments to leave a review at your favorite retailer. This is the only way for authors to get feedback regarding their work, and without it, improvements are difficult to make. Thank you for your continued support!

Glossary of Terms – an aid to non-military readers
Taken in part from Viet Nam Generation, Inc
Sixties Project, copyright (c) 1996

Actual: The unit commander. Used to distinguish the commander from the radioman when the call sign is used over the radio.

Advanced Individual Training: Specialized training taken after Basic Training, also referred to as AIT, i.e. infantry, cook school, armor, helicopters, artillery, etc.

Airborne: Refers to soldiers who are qualified to jump out of planes with chutes.

AK-47: Soviet combat assault rifle that fires a 7.62-mm round - primary weapon of VC / NVA

Ammo dump: Location where live or expended ammunition is stored in any compound

AO: Area of operations – designated area where an infantry unit will patrol through

APC: Armored personnel carrier. A tracked vehicle used to transport Army troops or supplies ARVN: Army of the Republic of Vietnam; the South Vietnamese Regular Army and US ally

Azimuth: A compass bearing to a set location or point of travel

B-40 rocket: A shoulder-held rocket-propelled grenade launcher also called RPG

B-52: U.S. Air Force high-altitude bomber – dropped 500# bombs leaving hundreds of craters.

Bandolier: A cloth cummerbund filled with two-hundred rounds of .223 caliber ammunition for the M16. Soldiers usually refill their magazines with these rounds and then store the filled magazines in the five pouches of the bandolier; laces on both ends allow the rifleman to secure it almost anywhere.

Basecamp: A large, permanent base in the "rear area" that supports brigade or division size units, artillery batteries and airfields. It is here where all new recruit training and standown occur, and where headquarters, mail, supplies, aircraft and ammo are stored.

Basic: Basic training – first eight weeks of military training when one enters the service.

Battalion: A military unit composed of a headquarters and two or more companies, batteries, or similar units comprised of 400 + personnel.

Beehive round: An artillery shell, containing thousands of small flechettes (nails with fins) that exit the barrel when the weapon fires. This mimics a shotgun. A 40mm version is also available for M79's.

Berm: Perimeter fortification comprised of bulldozed earth raised higher than the surrounding area - usually found surrounding smaller firebases.

Bird: Any aircraft, but usually refers to helicopters

Blasting cap: An electronic detonator similar in size to a short silver pencil - two-fifty foot long attached thin wires send an electrical charge to the cap – either by battery or manually via a detonation clacker. When exploding by itself, it sounds like a small firecracker.

Blood trail: A trail of blood left on the ground or vegetation by a wounded man, who is trying to get away. The amounts vary from periodic droplets to puddles.

Body bag: Thick, plastic, zippered bag used to transport dead bodies from the field.

Body count: The number of enemy killed, wounded, or captured during an operation. The term was used by

Washington and Saigon as a means of measuring the progress of the war.

Boony hat: Soft cloth hat with a brim, similar to a fishing hat, worn by infantry soldiers in the boonies.

Boonies: Infantry term for the field; jungles or swampy areas far from the comforts of civilization.

Bouncing Betty: Antipersonnel mine with two charges: the first propels the explosive charge upward, and the other is set to explode at about waist level.

Breaking squelch: Disrupting the natural static of a radio by depressing the transmit bar on another radio set to the same frequency, also called keying the mike.

Bro / Brother: A black soldier; also, at times, referencing fellow soldiers from the same unit

Bronze Star: U.S. military decoration awarded for heroic or meritorious service in combat

BS: Bullshit, as in chewing the fat, telling tall tales, or telling lies

Bummer: Bad luck, a real drag

Bush: Infantry term for the field

C-4: Plastic, putty textured explosive carried by infantry soldiers to blow up bunkers and weapon caches. When not compressed, it burns like sterno and was sometimes used to heat C-rations in the field.

Cache: Hidden supplies

C&C: Command and control helicopter used by reconnaissance or unit commanders

Cav: Cavalry; the 1st Cavalry Division (Airmobile)

Charlie: Viet Cong; the enemy

Cherry: Slang term for youth and inexperience; a virgin

Chinook: Twin bladed CH-47 cargo helicopter used to transport troops and equipment

Chop chop: Vietnamese slang for food

Chopper: Any helicopter

Chuck: Term used by black soldiers to identify white individuals; often derogatory

CIB: Combat infantry badge. An Army award received after coming under enemy fire in a combat zone.

Clacker: A small hand-held firing device for a claymore mine

Claymore: An antipersonnel mine carried by the infantry which, when detonated, propels small 25mm steel balls in a 60-degree fan-shaped pattern to a maximum distance of 100 meters.

Clearance: Permission from both military and political authorities to engage the enemy in a particular area – usually near populated areas.

Cobra: Narrow, two-man AH-1G attack helicopter / gunship, armed with rockets and machine guns.

Commo: Short for "communications"

Commo bunker: Bunker containing vital communications equipment normally within a battalion-sized firebase, where communications is maintained with all the battalion elements outside of the camp. Usually houses the Colonel and Executive Officer.

Commo wire: Communications wire similar to phone wire

Company: Military unit usually consisting of a headquarters and two or more platoons usually comprised of 150 + personnel.

Compound: Any fortified military installation

Concertina wire: Coiled barbed wire used as an obstacle and normally surrounding compounds

Contact: Engaged with the enemy in a firefight

C-rations: Combat rations. Canned meals for use in the field; each consisting of a basic course, a can of fruit, a

packet of some type of dessert, a packet of powdered coca, a four-pack of cigarettes, and two pieces of chewing gum.
CS: Riot-control gas which burns the eyes and mucus membranes

Dai uy: Vietnamese for captain
Dap: Handshake and greeting which may last up to ten minutes and is characterized by the use of both hands and often comprised of slaps and snaps of the fingers. Used by black soldiers, highly ritualized and unit specific.
Det-cord: White, rope like cord used with explosives or as a stand along
Deuce-and-a-half: Two-and-a-half ton truck – ten wheeler with cab and large bed used for transporting equipment and personnel; usually covered with a canvas roof.
Di-di: Leave quickly, running away
DMZ: Demilitarized zone. The dividing line between North and South Vietnam established in 1954 at the Geneva Convention.
Doc: Any medic or corpsman
Dust-off: Medical evacuation by helicopter

Elephant grass: Tall, razor-edged tropical plant that grows in dense clumps up to ten feet high. The grass is the favorite meal for elephants and also for feeding livestock and wildlife.
Eleven Bravo: The military occupation specialty description for an infantryman
E-tool: Entrenching tool. Folding shovel carried by infantrymen.
Evac'd: Evacuated

F-4: Phantom jet fighter-bombers. Range: 1,000 miles. Speed: 1400 mph. Payload: 16,000 lbs. The workhorse of the tactical air support fleet.

Fast mover: An F-4 jet

Fatigues: Standard combat uniform, green in color

FSB: Fire support base

Firebase: Temporary artillery encampment used for fire support of forward ground operations

Firefight: A battle or exchange of fire with the enemy

Flak jacket: Heavy fiberglass-filled vest worn for protection against shrapnel

Flare: Illumination projectile; hand-fired or shot from artillery, mortars, or dropped by aircraft. They float on parachutes and depending upon size, could last several minutes.

Flechette: A small dart-shaped projectile clustered in an explosive warhead. A mine without great explosive power containing small pieces of shrapnel intended to wound and kill.

FNG: Acronym for fucking new guy or cherry

Frag: Fragmentation grenade

Fragging: The assassination of an officer by his own troops, usually by a grenade

Freak: Radio frequency, also, a junkie or doper.

Freedom Bird: The plane taking soldiers from Vietnam back to the World after their tours end

Free fire zone: Designated zone where soldiers are free to fire upon suspected targets without having to await permission - area where everyone was deemed hostile and can be fired upon.

Friendly fire: Accidental attacks on U.S. or allied soldiers by other U.S. or allied soldiers

Fucked up: Wounded or killed, also, stoned, drunk, foolish or doing something stupid.

GI: Government issue. Usually refers to an American soldier or supplies owned by the military.

Gook: Derogatory term for an Asian, most often-used name for enemy soldiers

Grunt: Infantryman in Vietnam

Gung ho: Enthusiastic and ready to go

Gunship: Armed helicopter with rocket pods and side mounted miniguns.

H&I : Harassment and Intimidation - random artillery fire into suspected hostile areas to keep the enemy off balance.

Hard-stripe sergeant: Rank indicated by three chevron insignia, equivalent to an E5 – lowest grade of a non-commissioned officer.

Heart: Purple Heart award for a wound; the wound itself

Heat tabs: Flammable tablet used to heat C-rations that were always in short supply. These tabs were not a hot as C4 and took longer to cook a meal that wasn't as hot.

Ho Chi Minh sandals: Sandals made from tires. The soles are made from the tread and the straps from inner tubes. All VC and many local villagers wore these.

Hooch / Hootch: A hut or simple dwelling, either military or civilian where people can sleep.

Hoochgirl: Vietnamese woman employed by American military as maid or laundress

Horn: Radio microphone

Hot LZ: Landing zone under enemy fire

HQ: Headquarters

Huey: Nickname for the UH-1 series helicopters

Hump: March or hike carrying a rucksack and full supplies

Illum: Illumination flare, usually fired by a mortar or artillery weapon

Immersion foot: Condition resulting from feet being submerged in water for a prolonged period of time, causing cracking and bleeding. Also called jungle rot or trench foot.

In-country: Within the country of Vietnam

Iron Triangle: Viet Cong dominated area between the Thi-Tinh and Saigon rivers, next to Cu Chi district; an area laced with enemy supply trails, which transport goods into South Vietnam from the Ho Chi Minh trail in Cambodia.

Jungle boots: Footwear that looks like a combination of combat boot and canvas sneaker used by the U.S. military in a tropical climate, where leather rots because of the dampness. The canvas structure also speeds drying after crossing streams, rice paddies, etc.

Jungle penetrator: Winch and cable device used by Medevac helicopters to extract wounded soldiers from dense jungle locations where an LZ is not available. They are usually used in conjunction with either a seat or a flat platform where the patient is tied in and pulled up through the thick, overhead canopy and into the helicopter.

Jungle rot: Skin disease common in tropical climates. Symptoms are similar to trench foot and immersion foot where the skin cracks, itches, and blisters may form, followed by skin and tissue dying and falling off. This was difficult to treat because of the harsh tropical environment.

KIA: Killed in action

Kill zone: The radius of a circle around an explosive device within which it is predicted that 95 percent of all occupants will be killed should the device explode

Kit Carson scout: Former Viet Cong who act as guides for U.S. military units

Klick: Kilometer – one-thousand meters or six-tenths of a mile

KP: Kitchen police; mess hall duty

LAW: Shoulder-fired, 66-millimeter rocket, similar in effect to a 3.5-inch rocket, except that the launcher is made of Fiberglass, and is disposable after one shot

LBJ: Long Binh Jail, a military stockade on the Long Binh post

Lifer: Career military man. The term is often used in a derogatory manner.

Litters: Stretchers to carry dead and wounded

Loach: Small two passenger LOH helicopter used by military as decoys to lure the enemy into firing upon this small craft. Usually, they are part of a hunter-killer team, and after identifying the enemy, gunships attack the suspect area

LP: Listening post. A two or three-man position set up at night outside the perimeter away from the main body of troopers, which acts as an early warning system against attack.

LRRP: Long Range Reconnaissance Patrol. An elite team usually composed of five to seven men who go deep into the jungle to observe enemy activity without initiating contact.

L-T: Acronym for lieutenant and used primarily in the field

LZ: Landing zone. A clearing designated for the landing of helicopters. Used for combat assaults, resupply and medical evacuation.

M-16: Standard U.S. military rifle used in Vietnam from 1966 onward

M-60: Standard lightweight machine gun used by U.S. forces in Vietnam. It weighs twenty-three pounds and fires 7.62mm ammunitions – same as an AK-47.

M-79: U.S. military hand-held 40mm grenade launcher sometimes called a blooper

MA: Mechanical ambush - an American set booby trap using claymore mines.

Mad minute: An all-out weapons free-fire, used for testing weapons or firing into suspected enemy locations prior to an element sweeping through the area.

MARS: Military Affiliate Radio Station. Used by soldiers to call home via Signal Corps and ham radio equipment.

Marker round: First round fired by mortars or artillery, used for confirming a location on a map or an adjustment point when firing upon the enemy.

Mechanized platoon: A platoon operating with tanks and/or armored personnel carriers

Medevac: Medical evacuation from the field by helicopter

MIA: Missing in action

Minigun: Electronically controlled, extremely rapidly firing machine gun. Most often mounted on aircraft to be used against targets on the ground – similar to a Gatling gun.

Mortar: A muzzle-loading cannon with a short tube in relation to its caliber that throws projectiles with low muzzle velocity at high angles.

MOS: Military occupational specialty

MP: Military police
MPC: Military payment currency. The scrip U.S. soldiers were paid in.

Nam: Vietnam
Napalm: A jellied petroleum substance which burns fiercely, and is used as a weapon against personnel. The burst is so hot that the oxygen is literally removed from the air and some enemy soldiers had died from suffocation instead of the flames.
NCO: Noncommissioned officer, usually a squad leader or platoon sergeant.
NDP: Night defensive position where platoon-sized or larger units set-up sleeping and defensive positions in a circle. Claymore mines and trip flares are used outside of the perimeter and a guard position routinely positioned in the center where individuals rotate on hourly watches.
Net: Radio frequency setting, from "network."
No sweat: Slang for easy or simple
NVA: North Vietnamese Army – these soldiers complete formal training just like the Americans

Observation post: Similar to a listening post but implemented during the day

Papa san: Used by U.S. servicemen for any older Vietnamese man
Perimeter: Outer boundaries of a military position. The area beyond the perimeter belongs to the enemy.
PFC: Private first class – enlisted rank achieved usually after completing AIT
Pig: Slang for the M-60 machine gun. Belts of ammo were considered "pig food".

Platoon: A subdivision of a company-sized military unit, normally consisting of two or more squads or sections containing 40 + personnel

Point: The forward man or element on a combat patrol

Poncho: Five-foot square, plastic coated nylon poncho had a permanently attached hood in the center, and snap fasteners down both sides. Used as a rain cape, blanket, sleeping bag cover, ground cover for sleeping, tent half and litter to carry wounded soldiers.

Poncho liner: Thin, lightweight, nylon comforter used as a blanket or insert for a poncho.

Pop smoke: Request to ignite a smoke grenade to signal an aircraft.

PRC-25: Portable Radio Communications, Model 25. A back-packed FM receiver-transmitter used for short-distance communications. The range of the radio was 5-10 kilometers.

Prick 25: Slang for the PRC-25 radio

R&R: Short for rest and recreation, this is usually a three to seven-day vacation from the war for a soldier.

Red alert: The most urgent form of warning, this signals an imminent enemy attack.

REMF: Acronym for rear area support soldiers; infantry soldiers refer to them as (rear-echelon motherfuckers)

RIF: Reconnaissance in force.

Rome plow: Mammoth bulldozer used to flatten dense jungle and create berms on **perimeters**

ROTC: Reserve Officer's Training Corps. Program offered in many high schools and colleges, geared to prepare students to become military officers.

RPG: Rocket-propelled grenade, a Russian-made portable antitank grenade launcher.

RTO: Radio telephone operator, carries his unit's radio on his back in the field.

Ruck/rucksack: Backpack issued to infantry in Vietnam to carry rations and other supplies

Saddle up: Command given to put on one's pack and get ready to march

Sapper: A Viet Cong or NVA commando armed with explosives, his goal is to infiltrate defensive perimeters prior to a planned ground attack, opening lanes of attack for the enemy.

Satchel charges: Pack used by the enemy containing fused explosives that is dropped or thrown; they are powerful and can destroy bunkers and other equipment.

Search and destroy: An operation in which Americans searched an area and destroyed anything which the enemy might find useful

Shit burning: The burning of waste at remote firebase locations using kerosene and diesel fuel, this duty, considered the worst overall, was dreaded and looked upon as punishment.

Short: A term used by soldiers in Vietnam to signify that his tour was almost over

Short-timer: Soldier nearing the end of his tour in Vietnam

Shrapnel: Pieces of metal sent flying by an explosion, i.e. bomb, grenade, mortar, artillery.

Sit-rep: Short for a situation report, command personnel routinely contacted units in the field hourly for these updates

SKS: A Russian 7.62 mm semi-automatic carbine – not too many were used by the enemy.

Slackman: The second man on a patrol, following behind the point man to cover his back. He usually scans the treetops and flank areas; takes compass readings and counts steps.

Slick: UH-1 helicopter used for transporting troops in tactical air assault operations. The helicopter did not have protruding armaments and was, therefore, "slick".

Smoke grenade: A canister, armed similar to a grenade, emits brightly colored smoke after the contents are ignited by the blasting cap. They are available in various colors and used for signaling.

Spec-4: Specialist 4th Class. An Army rank immediately above Private First Class. Most enlisted men who had completed their individual training and had been on duty for a few months were Spec-4s, the most common rank in the Vietnam-era Army.

Spider hole: Camouflaged enemy foxhole with an overhead cover that raises and lowers after firing – sniper is well hidden and hard to find. Sometimes these holes are connected to small escape tunnels.

Squad: Small military unit consisting of less than ten men

Staff sergeant: E-6, the second lowest noncommissioned officer rank

Stand-down: An infantry unit's return from the boonies to the base camp for refitting, training and resting.**Starlight scope**: An image intensifier using reflected light to identify targets at night

Steel pot: The standard U.S. Army helmet. The steel pot is the outer metal cover that is sometimes used as a sink.

Steel Helmet insert: Fiberglass insert with straps and cushions that rest on a soldier's head – similar to a football helmet's inside. The steel pot fits over the top of this insert.

Strobe: Hand held strobe light for marking landing zones at night or identifying friendlies to overhead aircraft

Ti-ti: Vietnamese slang for a small amount or a little bit

Top: Nickname for a First Sergeant, the second highest non-commissioned officer rank

Tracer: A round of ammunition chemically treated to glow or give off smoke so that its flight can be followed. Belts of ammunitions for machine guns normally have every fifth round in the belt a tracer. When firing long bursts, the lighted round helps in adjusting the aim toward targets. Infantry soldiers usually load a couple of tracer rounds in their magazines; some only use them as a last round to signify an empty magazine. VC and NVA tracers are mostly green and USA is red.

Tracks: Any vehicles which move on tracks rather than wheels

Tree line: Row of trees at the edge of a field or rice paddy

Trip flare: A ground flare triggered by a trip wire used to signal and illuminate the approach of an enemy at night.

Tropic Lighting: The U.S. 25th Infantry Division

USO: United Service Organization. Provided entertainment to the troops, and was intended to raise morale.

VC: Viet Cong, the National Liberation Front

Victor Charlie: Military phonetic spelling for Viet Cong; the enemy.

Viet Cong: The Communist-led forces fighting the South Vietnamese government.

Wake-up: As in "13 and a wake-up" -- the last day of a soldier's Vietnam tour.

Walking wounded: Soldiers injured but still able to walk without assistance.

Web gear: Canvas belt and shoulder straps for packing equipment and ammunition on infantry operations – similar to a belt and suspenders.

Weed: Marijuana

White phosphorus: A type of explosive round from artillery, mortars, or rockets. The rounds exploded with a huge puff of white smoke from the hotly burning phosphorus, and were used as marking rounds or incendiary rounds. When white phosphorus hit the skin of a living creature it continued to burn until it had burned through the body. Water would not extinguish it.

WIA: Wounded in action

Willy Pete: Slang for white phosphorus

World, the: How soldiers referenced the United States and back home

XO: Executive officer; the second in command of a military unit

Zapped: Killed

About the author:

John Podlaski (1951 -) was raised in Detroit, Michigan and attended St. Charles and St. Thomas Apostle Catholic schools, graduating in 1969. Immediately afterward, John started working for one of the automotive parts suppliers in the area and then attended junior college full-time in the fall. After four months of overwhelming pressure, John dropped out of college - choosing income over education. This turned out to be a huge error in judgement as a school deferment protected him from the military draft. Uncle Sam wasted no time and Mr. Podlaski soon found himself inducted into the Army in February 1970. Then after six months of training, John was sent to Vietnam as an infantry soldier; serving with both the Wolfhounds of the 25th Division and the Geronimo of the 101st Airborne Division. During his tour of duty, John was awarded the Combat Infantry Badge, Bronze Star, two Air Medals, the Vietnamese Cross of Gallantry, and several other campaign medals. Back in the states, Mr. Podlaski spent the next four months in Fort Hood, Texas before receiving an early military discharge in December 1971.

The War Veteran returned to his former position with the automotive supplier and because of his military experience, he was promoted to shift supervisor. He met Janice Jo a few months later and married in 1973. The G.I. Bill helped them to purchase a home in Sterling Heights, MI, they continue living there to this day. A daughter, Nicole Ann was born in 1979. Using additional benefits from the G.I. Bill, Mr. Podlaski returned to college part time; graduating four years later with an Associate Degree in Applied Science.

In 1980, John began working on his memoir about his Vietnam experiences. He had carried a diary during his year in Vietnam, and his mother had saved all the letters he had written from the war zone - both were used to create the outline. He toiled on a manual typewriter for four years before finally completing his work. About the same time, a new national veteran group, akin to the V.F.W. was formed in Washington, DC. They called themselves "Vietnam Veterans of America" and chapters quickly sprung up around the country. John joined Chapter 154 in Mt. Clemens, MI, and as an active member, helped to launch their inaugural Color Guard - marching in parades and posting colors for local events. The members of this chapter were a closely knit group, but wives often felt left out during the many discussions about Vietnam. When learning that John had authored a book about his tour of duty, the wives asked to share a copy of the manuscript, hoping it would help them better understand what their husbands might have endured during their time in Vietnam. The memoir was well received, and wives were now joining their men during these discussions. All were increasingly supportive and urged him to locate a publisher. After hundreds of rejections, a publisher from Atlanta, GA finally came forward and offered to consider the manuscript if it were re-written to a third-person format.

Atari had just come out with a new computer console and a word processor - making re-writes and editing much easier; his work now saved on floppy diskettes. The re-write continued until 1989, consuming all his spare time. John had finished half of the manuscript, then suddenly lost interest - discouraged, and not wanting to work on it any longer - it was ten years already and there was no light at the end of the tunnel. So everything was boxed up and moved to the garage for storage.

Mr. Podlaski continued working for various companies within the automotive sector; primarily in Management roles tasked in either plant start-ups, financial turnaround, or plant closures. John returned to college in 2000 and received a Bachelor Degree in Business Administration two years later. He and his wife retired in mid-2013.

At John's 40th high school reunion, many of his former classmates who read his original manuscript twenty years earlier had questioned its lack of publication. It was a great story and all were relentless in their efforts to get him motivated and finish the rewrite - offering help wherever needed.

After learning that the conversion of Atari diskettes to the Microsoft Word format was extremely cost prohibitive, John's daughter offered to retype both the completed manuscript and the rewrite, saving both on a USB memory stick. Nine months later, "Cherries" was completed and published. It took almost thirty years, but seeing it in print made it all worthwhile.

During his retirement, John published a second book about his Vietnam experience called, "*When Can I Stop Running?*" in 2016. Additionally, he's published two short stories: *Unhinged* and *Unwelcomed*; all are available on Amazon.

The author and his wife, Jan, live in Sterling Heights, Michigan and care for their new and only granddaughter while mom works. They also own a 1997 Harley Davidson Heritage motorcycle and enjoy riding when possible; both

John Podlaski

are members of the Harley Owner Group. This is his fifth published book.

Other books by this author:

Cherries: A Vietnam War Novel: This is a painfully accurate description of the life of a combat infantryman serving in the jungles of Vietnam. It portrays, in sometimes chilling detail, the swings he experienced between stifling boredom and utter terror that made up the life of this often-unappreciated soldier. The narrative is compelling, and the storytelling is excellent throughout. If you want to know what these young and not so young men saw and felt, this will help you gain a bit of understanding of the sacrifices they made.

The e-book version remained within the top 100 of the Amazon Top Seller lists in its category since its inception in 2010.

On January 21, 2013, PageOneLit dot com named *Cherries - A Vietnam War Novel* by John Podlaski - *BEST AUDIOBOOK OF 2012.* This was a proud moment for John Podlaski - recipient of the ***"Books and Authors Award for Literary Excellence".***

When notified by contest officials of his good fortune in winning the audiobook category, the e-mail included the following quote from one of the contest judges, **"One HELL of a book!!!"**

Find it here:
https://www.amazon.com/Cherries-Vietnam-Novel-John-Podlaski-ebook/dp/B003R4Z5U6

When Can I Stop Running? A Vietnam War Story:
Outstanding read that paints a dramatic picture of what it was like to man an LP (listening post) in enemy territory on a night that never seems to end. Interwoven with the story is flashbacks from the author's youth when terrifying events scared him into running for his life. But now, in the darkness, a short distance from the enemy, he cannot run. He must stay at his assigned station, maintain total silence, and report enemy activities to his headquarters.

It is one thing to read that our soldiers were sent from their outposts, in teams of two, to maintain reconnaissance of the enemy territory. It is quite another to learn the intimate details of what that entailed. This book paints a graphic picture of everything involved in LP duty - constant mosquito bites, sitting in a mud hole being pelted by rain, hearing (and smelling) enemy soldiers taking their latrine breaks mere feet away.

The descriptions are extremely well-crafted and vivid, and the flashbacks might evoke memories from your own reckless youth.

This book is also the prequel to the book you just finished.

Find it here:

https://www.amazon.com/When-Can-I-Stop-Running-ebook/dp/B01H9BESNC

Unhinged – A Micro Read: Two fourteen-year-old boys are offered a great first-time opportunity to watch a movie by themselves at a local drive-in theater. Little did they realize that the movie would affect them in ways neither imagined nor will ever forget.

Find it here:

https://www.amazon.com/Unhinged-Micro-Read-John-Podlaski-ebook/dp/B089LGHPZJ

Unwelcomed: A Short Story - John Kowalski makes it home from the Vietnam War in one piece, and his battles are finally over. Or so he thought. Home for less than a week, John must defend his family from a pair of unwelcomed thugs hell-bent on revenge.

Find it here:

https://www.amazon.com/Unwelcomed-Short-Story-John-Podlaski-ebook/dp/B08GY46XGZ

Made in United States
Orlando, FL
13 June 2022

18756463R00090